Good Night, Jenny

Mike Pfau

PublishAmerica
Baltimore

© 2008 by Mike Pfau.
All rights reserved. No part of this book may be reproduced, stored in a retrieval system or transmitted in any form or by any means without the prior written permission of the publishers, except by a reviewer who may quote brief passages in a review to be printed in a newspaper, magazine or journal.

First printing

All characters in this book are fictitious, and any resemblance to real persons, living or dead, is coincidental.

PublishAmerica has allowed this work to remain exactly as the author intended, verbatim, without editorial input.

ISBN: 1-60610-945-6
PUBLISHED BY PUBLISHAMERICA, LLLP
www.publishamerica.com
Baltimore

Printed in the United States of America

For my wife

Good Night, Jenny

Prologue

It was mid-afternoon on the narrows between Kabetogema and Namakan Lake, a windless, sun-stripped day when tempers could flare like fire in the marshland. Each summer ran a similar string when high pressure rolled in and boundary waters walleye men knew to break for a brew in the back booth of Bert's Pub where a poker game might be raging, or within Bertram's shaded walkway where spindle rockers were strung like loungers on the deck of a Caribbean liner. On the beach, children played in the sand, oblivious to the heat, content to while away their time building sand castles or teasing their siblings, with mothers looking on and keeping score with ultimatums like, *"Morgan Mae, you remember what I said. Watch out for your brother."* Or, *"How many times must I tell you not to throw mud in Levi's hair?"* Then Morgan would run like she owned the world and Levi would chase after her, his diaper heavy with *soil* and wet sand, and mother would sigh in resignation.

In the out-woods and on the high water, apart from the manicured resorts and beach parks, the outback remained sticky-thick with mosquitoes and gnats; and for the Currie boys, ignorant of brew or ships or *poop* decks, there lingered some bad memories, the moment compressed with emotion—*their mother gone, their island home now lost*—that strained for relief.

The boys should have avoided their real estate *investment* today, for just beyond the brink, irrationality lay waiting like a rusted number fourteen Newhouse, its pan-and-trigger honed fine and set to snap at provocation. Such was that afternoon mood when brothers Nels and Eddie landed in simple ignorance with their meager possessions, *and in grave danger,* on the mossy end of Big Timber, and when they were presently joined by a rogue realtor named Percy Greenwall.

Everyone knew Percy was a cheat, his practices intolerably common: *it was simply his way of doing things.* Most locals avoided him with *real* business to conduct, warning outsiders and newcomers whenever they could; but he was a slippery *agent* who could show-and-fade with regularity, and who could talk a streak when dollars were involved. *Unfortunately, few realized that Percy was a murderer, too.*

Likened to an island, their quarter-mile-long peninsula was one of many wooded extensions marking the broken southern shores of Kabetogema Lake. The area, *the islands,* was a fusion of bedrock outcrops, large and small; and even for those familiar with the maze, confusion was common, with spruce and pine and cedar bough abounding within an homogenized mix of bays, passages, and invitations to getting lost.

The brothers, unsettled, were unhappy with Percy, Nels shuffling his feet, kicking at pine cones and loose stones with the toes of his loggers nearly worn to the steel, and muttering inconsistencies like, "...the big dummy," and, "...mom never liked him very much, *did* she, Eddie," with Eddie hanging behind mimicking a reluctant tag-along on opening day of school, while their mottle-faced *agent*, sporting jacket and tie, presented a picture of condescension and impatience, the *businessman* having little time for *these* two. With more profitable pockets to pick, he was gearing for the *big* money; and he was in a hurry.

Percy wasn't new to Kabetogema. His family resided on Ash River until he was seventeen—*when they were compelled to leave*, he would claim—*when they were forced away*, he would squeal like a stuck swine to anyone naive enough to listen. *But they weren't forced away at all.* In fact, many family friends insisted they stay in Minnesota, and a good number were disappointed when the Greenwalls left *in spite* of their support. His father was accused of bank fraud *twenty years ago*; and for those who thought best that they relocate, it wasn't for the alleged *wrongs* old Greenwall had done because *there had been none;* rather, it was the inaccurate print in tabloids and on coffeehouse blurb boards that threatened to damage the family's reputation.

That much was true.

Condemned only by an ignorant few, the family had plenty of supporters. Despite being *run off*, as Percy loved to whine, it didn't matter that his father made good in Chicago. *It didn't matter* because Percy was determined to avenge the imagined wrongs done to his family and to *his own* reputation, and to wreak havoc on those who stole his Jenny away.

His Jenny, indeed.

For starters, *his Jenny* was gone for good. *Percy made certain of that by transporting her to the bottom of Namakan Narrows on the short end of a boat anchor.* And it made no difference that she knew him only affably. In fact, *she was Ted Snelling's wife.*

But Percy's *bizarrerie* had taken root: *he was crazy.* Complimented by his well-known self-centeredness, and likened to a flock of drunken bantams, his emotions resembled a free-for-all within his coconut-shaped warehouse of delusion, and led to this ill-omened meeting with the boys this afternoon.

"Y-you said we're ready to move in, Percy," Nels protested, his young face flushed red, his blue eyes wild. Slightly slumped over and canted to one side as he stood there—*he even leaned as he walked*—like the weight of the world on his young shoulders, he rather inclined toward Percy, as if appealing to a higher authority. Looking at Nels, peering into his eyes, it was like looking into a flock of bluebirds that had nowhere to land.

Nels and his brother had lived in the woods all their lives as jack-pine pulpers and fishing guides. They knew plenty about wildlife and survival, but they knew nothing of Percy. They knew *nothing* of his dark side, or of how he'd been tormented in school (Percy had few friends as he grew up, so the three of them had *something* in common) by all the bullies and misguided jocks who were ignorant of the misanthrope they were unwittingly molding and whose proud parents were as guilty as the bullies they babied.

Like everyone else, the brothers knew *of* Percy, like their mother knew *of* him, *of the beleaguered Greenwall family.*

She knew the Greenwalls were good people who felt compelled to leave the boundary waters, and she knew of the banker's young son who'd struggled in school because of a naiveté that bordered on stupidity. But she knew little of his being slapped on the face by turncoats, *even by his own sister who loathed him,* then falling impossibly introverted when *run out of the country,* as he loved to claim. *She knew nothing of the damage done to him when he was young, the bullying and the intimidation, or of the resulting ruination of Percy's pride, a fragile commodity to start with.* She was as unaware of his absolute corruption as were any of the innocents in the forest around.

"This ol' sh-shack ain't n-nothin'," Nels *spit* on the ground, an aberrant show of contempt that startled his own brother. *It wasn't like his brother to spit on the ground.* "It ain't been n-nothin' in y-years, I bet," he waved in renewed defiance while standing within the doorway of the rundown business he and Eddie had purchased in a transaction they'd been counseled against. *Be careful for Percy,* their friends had warned, with watchful words from Ted, as well. *He'll cheat you,* they'd advised, realizing Percy's reputation for misrepresentation and of his penchant for foul deeds.

Despite all-around cautions, the brothers—*Nels in particular, for he was the improbable business mind of the pair*—were not as careful as they should have been. This was unremarkable because they'd had no experience in the business world, and there wasn't a soul on the lakes who would cheat them. *Except for Percy Greenwall.*

Purchasing it by mail with the help of a local notary, *simply reviewing it from memory,* they hadn't seen their new place in months. The *last* time around, Nels remembered *a happier spot.* He remembered it in far better shape, too. And the boys expected it should remain that way. *A year ago* when traveling through with their mother, it *was* in fair repair, with old Bill chattering like a crazed tree squirrel about selling his home and bait shop and moving South. *He talked and laughed about selling it to anyone unsuspecting enough to buy it.* Of course, the boys didn't hear *that* part, and Bill had no way of knowing they'd eventually move in, nor could Mother Currie anticipate as much. The native grass had been cut back then, the pine cones gathered, the split-pine porch oil-sealed, and the place picked-up for presentation. Loose shingles, *those that were visible,* were replaced, and broken windows on the entrance side repaired. Inside, old Bill had whitewashed the Great Room and re-mortared the corner fireplace, making the building presentable, proper, and even homey in his bachelor-styled way.

But Bill, *in his bachelor-styled way,* was never married. And for good reason. There wasn't a woman in the entire north woods willing to put up with his penny-pinching compromises. *Nothing was ever done properly.* The last time through, Nels and Eddie had come away packing a rickety-clack sack of tackle that old Bill would never normally part with, and an undeniable clue that he was clearing out. *But that was a year ago.* And the tight-fisted loner—*Whisky Bill,* some called him, his weakness for Kentucky bourbon—hadn't put a dime into it since; so with Greenwall at the helm, the place hadn't a prayer of a legitimate sale.

"L-look around you, Percy. The b-building is fallin' apart. Ain't that right, Eddie," Nels regarded his brother, gathering him in as if lassoing a nervous colt for halter, at which Eddie, whose feet kept moving in place and going nowhere, nodded wide-eyed and unbelieving. "It ain't n-nothing like what it used to be," he challenged the real estate man. "It's one b-big damn mess now, ain't it Eddie," he pushed his words, like shoving them through a sausage stuffer, a steady stream to stop stammering.

Upon entering the building, Nels was pressed to an even deeper low. Casting his eyes about, he grew dark and began kicking at things, at the furniture, at the chromed leg of an ancient dining table too large for the room, at a cast-iron tinder-rack overstacked with cooking wood cut seasons ago, then at a deerantlered magazine stand stuffed with newspapers, dusty and months dry and bedecked with lacings of spider webs like at a Halloween hop.

At the center of the room was a pair of back-to-back but uncoordinated leatherette loungers, one *apparently* richer and darker than the other, each with an end stand and gas lamp atop; and at the foot of the chairs were placed round, cloth-braided *Cherokee* rugs cheaply *Made in China*. Newer than the rest, they were the only matching items throughout.

Then came more stammering, the dimple of Nels's chin set deep, the cords in his neck strung strong from cheek to chest, a habit he'd developed when warding off bad thoughts or protecting Eddie from aggressive visitors. Nels was upset with Percy; but he was even more frustrated with himself because he felt he'd let his brother down, that he'd led him astray with this imprudent purchase, and little he could do to repair his error. He tried reasoning with Percy when Eddie wasn't watching, but that fell short; and when his anemic, last-ditch threats were met with ridicule like, "...Who do you think you're talking to? You think I'm some kind of fool?" Nels grew dark and embarrassed and *more* chord tightening. *Who was the fool,* he wondered as he withdrew, the backwoods boy with no concept of suit-and-tie. Finally, at breaking point, he picked up a galvanized water bucket, sending the antique bounding across the wood-planked floor where, like an errant soccer ball, it crashed into an empty display case near the business end of the building, nearly shattering its glass front-piece already fractured from years of misuse but held together by fifty-year-old glue-backed ads for war-time savings bonds.

Percy stared at Nels with simmering indignation, determined that it would be the *last* of his outbursts. *He would put up with only so much of that kind of behavior.* That Saint Paul attorney with the pretty moustache and slicked back black hair found out how much Percy Greenwall would put up with, except the young law peddler, with his leather law books in hand, and who was *obviously* sent out here to watch him, was too proud to back off. He never caught on to Percy's *dark* side until it was too late. Hah!...Until he was sinking to the bottom of Sullivan Bay with six feet of log chain wrapped around his pompous neck. And *before that* when Jenny Snelling threatened to turn him in for cheating his clients who were *friends of hers*...bet she was surprised when her old boyfriend turned the tide! *"I'll report you, Percy! I'll do it! I mean it!"*

she'd warned, even while fighting him off. Let's see her report *that* to the authorities, Percy simmered. Then, *"Ted will find out,"* and, *"he'll be after you. He'll come looking for you,"* she'd threatened after realizing he'd had enough of her grousing; then, "You'll be going to jail," she'd pleaded when the warnings failed, when he bound her hands behind her back and tied a boat anchor to her feet; and finally, "I thought we were friends," she'd cried—*hah!*—in final desperation, those big brown eyes staring up at him as her pretty little face bobbed to the surface *one more time* then disappeared into the depths of the lake. But it was *her own fault*, he'd steeled himself. *She went too far*, he'd grimaced. And Ted never found out, either. There would be no Percy Greenwall *going to jail* like she'd warned. And he and Jenny were no longer best friends.

"Y-you said we could move right in. Y-you said, 'we're set for b-business.' What are me an' Eddie supposed to do around here, Percy?" Nels waved his arms helplessly about. "We're not set for no b-business. There ain't n-nothing in here to sell 'c-cause Mr. Lawman gave it all away," he pointed. "A-an' you said there'd be customers, Percy. Where are all the c-customers like you promised? Where are all the people coming by a-an' visiting like when they used to, like when we were here before," he reflected, but quieted, now stringing his words in an open display of the longing he and his brother felt for friends and family and familiar surroundings. "You said that—"

"Aw, 'you said…*you said*'. What do you want me to do? Huh? *What do you want from me, Nels?* I've done everything I could for you," he charged, then held back for fear of antagonizing Nels any further. Captured only by the young man's outburst, while ignorant of *either* boys' *real* emotions, he glared in refrain. Unable to understand their loneliness (Percy had known loneliness like no one else could), his contempt for the undiscerning brothers was impossibly shallow.

Percy felt his ability to manipulate more profitable *gullibles* was squandered on these two…*a useless effort. This was all he understood.* His talents were wasted on these backward boys, this pair of lake locals who'd never graced the inside of a high school or driven a car or experienced the clamor and clash of big-city streets and, *after tonight,* Percy simmered, *they likely never would.*

Nels Currie was two years older and more *difficult* than his brother. But Nels listened to Eddie, the slow one. Whenever Eddie struggled or needed advice, Nels was by his side like his mother had been. How far back? When he was a child, Eddie was stricken with a water-borne bug and a sickness *most* fended off with rest and treatment. But Eddie wasn't so lucky. Nels *knew* he'd had proper care and *he knew* it wasn't mom's fault he'd gotten so sick. But she blamed herself. "If we didn't live in the middle of nowhere," she would lament, "none of this would be…," and Nels could do little to comfort her.

Eddie recovered—*he didn't die*—but the infection weakened him. He would never hold down a job or live alone. Until a year ago, it was mom who listened and provided; but Mother Currie was gone now. She simply passed away in her sleep *without even saying goodbye*. And Eddie missed her terribly.

Over the years, she'd become endeared to Big Timber, to this island-like retreat, and to this never-to-be business Percy unloaded on her boys. So it was natural that Eddie would grow attached, too. It wasn't the business that attracted her, rather it was the solitude that Lawman's provided, the way it was set into an outcrop of rock protecting it from the trades that wore lesser buildings down, a cove-like beach-and-border reminding her of home. Nels understood this attraction, no matter that Ted advised him that the business no longer had electricity, its power lines flooded out and fallen into disrepair; it had poor water, no land approach, and was *a bad bargain all around*.

Despite her attachment to the peninsula, Mother Currie would agree with Ted about *the Park* putting places like Lawman's out of business and the changes turning the boundary waters into a moneyed playground. No, she'd have *never* purchased Bill's spot on Big Timber. *Not now.* Not the way old Bill had let it fall into a patched-up bait shop with a bed-in-back and bathhouse on the beach.

But who could blame old Bill? "I'm no politician," he would complain to his friends and to the stragglers holding on. Like everyone else, he saw the changes coming. So like everyone else, he absconded when year-'rounders began dropping out. *"What else can I do?"* he appealed. After he left, he had no way to anticipate the Currie boys' *arrival* and, *like Mother Currie,* there was no way *he'd* have allowed the sale with Percy Greenwall pulling strings: Bill may have been a cheapskate, but he wouldn't cheat the boys.

It was near Kubel Island on the eastern end of Namakan Narrows as the border bends toward Kettle Falls where the boys and their mom lived. She refused to move after her husband, a civil engineer, died in a landslide on a highway building project west of Buyck. The boys were too young to know him very well; but he was on the road most of the time, anyway. Their island, *Currie Island*, was wooded and pristine and even *without* dad around, it was a great place to grow up and perfect for them all.

At least until last year, it was perfect.

With the government reclaiming leased boundary-water property for the new park, Eddie and Nels had to leave their island behind. Years ago, when plans for the Park had been set into law, *original* lease holders could either sell back their contracts or they could stay on as long as they lived; but because mom was now gone, the law was clear: *the brothers had to move.*

But...*to where do they move?* Their old home was miles from the station and friends, and in waters more remote than the popular Daley Bay of Kabetogema from where Percy ran his business and to where the boys headed for occasional supplies.

Where they stood wasn't *home*, but Big Timber was the *one spot* Eddie remembered as his mother's "...most favorite place this side of civilization." Nevertheless, Nels was disappointed. More dilapidated, more run-down than he remembered, he realized they'd been cheated. Despite Eddie's memories, *he knew* they'd paid Percy too much.

"There's everything you need here," Percy gestured encouragement; but his was a pitiable act, a lackluster show, for the bait shop was beyond repair and profit, a poor bargain, and worth far less than what the boys had paid. And the young men knew it too. A*t least Nels did.* But because he feared the boys would run for help the first chance they got, Percy kept trying: "You got a fridge and a stove—*look here,*" he pointed to a tottering, shuddering, gas-run Coolerator that looked ready to give up the world even as a puddle of yellowed condensation formed beneath it and pooled out over the floor, then to the tarnish-torn table and chairs left behind, and the sagging cupboards with doors cracked and warped ajar, hinges rusted and worn. "I bought groceries for you," he offered. "You got your own well out back, and I even hooked up the generator last week," he dramatized, despite the generator being unreliable and rarely used; and with power on the peninsula, it wouldn't have been needed at all. But he wasn't ready to return their money. Besides, he no longer had a dime of it. "There ain't nothin' wrong 'round here some hard work won't fix. You boys afraid of a little work? A little elbow grease?" he gamely challenged. *"What would your mom say to that?"* a patronizing glimmer, an evil twist of his lips and a crick in his voice that made the forest shudder and the spirit of Kabetogema turn in his grave.

"But you said it was all set," Nels rejoined, weaker this time, his head tilted to one side and lowered to a pout, Percy's argument taking hold.

"Look...," spacing his words, he painted his charm with a contemptuously conciliatory string, like with cheap oils on green wood, "you two stick it out for a few days. Make yourself comfortable, make yourself at home," he narrowed evil. "What do you say? You give the old place a chance. And after that, if you're not happy, *if you don't like it here,* I'll write out a check for the whole amount. *I'll refund every cent.* I'll even give you cash if you want," he put his arm around the older brother, as if manipulating a child. *"What do you think about that?"*

"I don't know," Nels retreated, his clenched fists stuffed into his pockets like gripping a pair of pine cones. He was still upset, but secretly eyeing Eddie now, for Eddie was all he cared about. In many ways, Eddie *was* a child. *He even appeared a child.* Slow and withdrawn, Eddie had been his mother's special boy, and he was Nels's constant companion since she passed away.

"—*All of it,*" Percy insisted, catching Nels's direction, adjusting his attention, a sadistic shift in his manners. "How can you go wrong? *Look,* even Eddie likes the place, *don't you, Eddie,*" he appealed, at which Eddie replied with a self-conscious shrug, the curious half-smile that broke whenever he was embarrassed. Then returning to Nels, he continued, "Doesn't it matter what Eddie wants? *Doesn't it matter that he likes the place?*" Percy tried his own smile, but it was a crooked contrivance, unbalanced and evil.

"Well, what d'you think, Eddie," Nels softened, hopefully

regarding his brother, all the while unimpressed and unmoved by Percy's tactics. Nels no longer had faith in Percy nor in the venture this fast-talker saddled them with. He simply *wanted* it to work. He felt obligated to his brother to make a go of it. And he felt a need to do right by his mother because Eddie was *his* charge now; and *this*, this land of lakes and pines and rugged isolation was the only life they knew, the only life that Eddie could identify with. So what could he do but *try* to *make* it work?

Eddie shrugged, a veiled consent at which his hands were *also* thrust into the pockets of his overalls, a self-conscious introversion mirroring his brother's, and at which Percy echoed:

"*Good! Then it's for sure!* I'll be back in a week to see how you two make out."

But it wasn't a week.

In fact, *that same night,* Percy idled his boat, a sleek, red, inboard runabout, a completely useless and out-of-place craft on these northern waters, into a rock-lined bay called *The Shoals*, a popular early-spring fishing spot a hundred yards south of the boys' place on the privately owned peninsula called Big Timber. It was late, it was dark, and it was warm. The night was calm; and there was no moon, and no fishermen this deep into the evening. But the stars danced brightly and the northern lights shimmered their ironic *all is well* across the diamond-studded blackness, rendering the rugged waterline crystal sharp and easy to follow.

Percy quietly eased his way along the half-submerged boulders and rocky barriers making up most of the shoreline, presently tying out of sight to a decaying, little-used dock well below the white-gas window lights of the bait shop, and far from the landing that the boys *and Bill* always used. There he deliberated: *in his mind he'd traveled this path before.* But his path had no end, no outcome, his *stealth* a behavior he had no control over, like an opportunistic burglar skulking about in the darkness in search of a windfall. He knew the brothers were alone. *He knew that.* And he knew they'd had supper and were set to turn in, for they had nothing else to do. At least, that's what he *thought* he knew. They had no radio. *He was certain of that.* So *how else* might they occupy their time? After all, how much could they carry in their miserable fishing boat? Completely ignorant of Nels's library, a case of books his mother left him and to which friends had added from time-to-time, and of Eddie's rudimentary efforts at landscape painting, and to the coin collection his father began, Percy could fathom only the notion of *worth* in his imaginary looking glass, or in the *fleecibility* of gullible buyers—*or in the value of a dollar bill.*

The boys had few neighbors, and Lawman's Landing was never a mainstream tourist haven to begin with, rather a spot where fishermen might stop for bait, for refreshments, and where locals would congregate for news and gossip before the boundary waters were forced into park land, *before traffic into Lawman's was reduced to a trickle, and land values on Big Timber fell to a fraction of what the boys had paid.* So a visitor this time of night was the *last* they'd expect, and the re-arrival of Percy Greenwall was the farthest thing from their minds. *But the boys didn't know Percy, and they knew nothing of the evil howling about the vacant hollow which once housed his soul.*

Grabbing his pearl-handled pistol, a completely out-of-place firearm in this country, even as he stuffed a familiar role of construction tape into his coat pocket, Percy stumbled up through the trees toward the shop, tripping in his street shoes over rocks and deadfall, slipping and falling like an amateur *sidewalker* onto low-lying juniper lining the pathway, slapping and brushing away mosquitoes as he bumbled along. He had neither plans nor an outline of a mission tonight; he had only the confidence of past successes and an evil resolve whirling dervishly in his mind to keep his terrible spree going strong. The boys were a threat now, just as Jenny Snelling and that attorney had been threats, and he had no intention of allowing them—*the boys*—to disrupt his operation, either.

"Hello in there! *Nels! Eddie!*" he bellowed from below. "We need your help out here," he found himself improvising, his contrived urgency confused and concealed by his cigarette-inspired huffing and wheezing and by his flair for deception.

The door opened. "Who's there? *Percy?*" Eddie poked his nose through. Eddie never said much, but he was excited to have company. *Any* company. "What are you doing here, Percy? We didn't hear your boat come in. We didn't hear you coming."

The boys knew his raucous voice. But aside from the deal they'd just struck, they had no reason to fear him or to assume his reappearance was evilly inspired. Although Percy had a questionable reputation (Their friends up the lake, warned them often about Percy's reputation, that he couldn't be trusted. But *trust* had no antonym for Nels and Eddie, no cause for caution), he was a mild-mannered, red-freckled fixture, well known for his manipulative and caustic personality; but for the boys, *violence* was unknown and impossible.

"Is that you, Percy?" Nels followed. "What are you doing back here?" he repeated. I thought you were gone. I thought you went on home tonight. Did you have supper yet? Are you alone tonight?" he peered innocently down the path for more guests.

"Yeah, it's me, all right. *Just me.* I've been back-and-forth on the water all evening," he lied. "Better get your brother out here, Nels—*no time for supper,"* he returned with pretentious excitement. *"And hurry it up,"* he urged, "because Ted needs your help. *There's been a fire at the sawmill,"* he lied some more, surprising himself with his extemporaneous string of cock-and-bull.

"A *fire?"* Eddie echoed. "A *big* fire?" he asked excitedly.

"Yeah, *a big one,* alright. We got it out O.K. But Ted's worried about flare-ups, and we need volunteers to keep watch." Proud of his fabrication, Percy continued the production. *No way to turn back now.*

Suspecting nothing, the boys were eager to help, for Ted was their friend; so the two grabbed their caps and jackets and followed Percy who outpaced them toward the water, his back turned, his gun hidden, his mind a cauldron of evil. Then, halfway to their dock, he spun around and snarled—*or tried to*—but like an unbalanced tilt-a-top, he nearly fell over; and like a worn out carnival barker, his voice cracked unconvincingly, almost comically: *"Stop right there!"* he squawked.

At first, Nels thought he was joking, and he almost laughed until Percy threw the roll of tape at him:

"Wrap your brother's hands—in front of him!" he snapped.

"What the hell. *What are you talking about? What's this for?"* Nels protested, a step closer, his smile dissolved. Percy wasn't funny anymore. "I thought you s-said there was a *f-fire."* he began to stutter again.

"There's no fire, Nels?" Eddie lisped from behind his brother, a weak interrogation. "Percy said there was a fire at the sawmill. He said Ted needed our help. Percy said that—"

"No, Eddie," Nels replied softly, "Ted doesn't need our help. And there's no fire at all."

"But Percy said that—"

"No, Eddie."

"But Percy said that—"

"Now!" Percy exploded, his face flushed, ashamed of himself. *"You hear me?"* he croaked as if frustrated with unmanageable children. Hacking a cigarette cough, he thrust his gun at them as he motioned toward the shore.

Nels obeyed, while his brother was confused and afraid. But Nels had no choice. As if in a nightmare, he had no way to explain to Eddie the evil he felt in Percy's presence and in his voice, even as Ted's caution haunted him with renewed meaning. He had no way to argue with Percy's pistol and with his foul resolve. There was no one out here to help them, for this was a *new* Percy they were witnessing, the *unpredictable* Percy that Ted cautioned them about, *the Percy with a tarnished soul;* and Nels wished he'd listened more closely to the warnings of his friends on the river.

While Nels taped, Percy ordered, "We're going to Ted's, and we're going to iron out this *mess* of yours," he repeated Nels' earlier condemnation of the place, even while waving the muzzle of his revolver toward the property he'd sold them last week.

"Yeah? Well, th-then why all th-this? Why the g-gun?" Nels alternated between his clumsy taping job and his focused accusations past his brother's worried face. "Why the middle of the n-night," he stuttered. "Why did you l-lie to Eddie about a f-fire?"

Eddie, standing with his back to Percy, looked back over his own shoulder, a shared expression whenever Nels led the way, like *two* sad thespian faces. Eddie was wide-eyed and Nels was frightened, both expecting the worst; they had not seen this side of Percy Greenwall; they'd never considered that he would *harm* anyone; and the warnings of their friends returned.

"Because I don't trust you."

"Because *you* don't trust *us*?" This time it was Eddie who interjected with a rare exclamation. "You're going to kill us, aren't you, Percy. You're going to throw us in the cold water," Eddie struggled, dwelling on each word, his face now turned full toward their antagonist. *"I don't like you anymore, Percy."* He seldom expressed himself this way; he rarely spoke with anyone but Nels, his own outburst too much for himself to bear, his fragile composure and simple trust ruptured wide; so when he turned back to his brother and started to cry, Nels was crushed, lost for words. *What could he do?* Eddie wasn't very strong. He was a quiet boy who was always easily intimidated.

"Don't be silly. I've got nothing against you," Percy tried to soften, a clumsy, shameful effort he knew he'd best abort.

Indeed, Eddie Currie was right. While leaving the gas lamps in the store to burn out on their own, and the pot of coffee on the stove to turn cold, he and Percy sat at the back of the boat as Nels navigated his own craft through the dark water and up the channel toward the pulsating blue beacon marking Ted Snelling's home on Rocky Point. Halfway there, Percy ordered him to stop....

Like Jenny, their bodies, as well as the remains of that *nosey attorney* from the cities last year, would never be found. Percy would make sure of that. He was learning to cover his tracks well.

Chapter 1

"You remember them, Mary," Owen Peterson slapped the evening Tribune with the back of his hand as if swatting at an annoying fly. "This paper makes 'em out as *bums*," he grumped. "If you didn't know any better, you'd think they were *thieves*," he slouched his pouching frame into the cushion of his leather recliner, with a cup of coffee at hand and his feet propped high on an old herringbone hassock Mary threw out twice since last fall, not realizing Owen had bargained with the trash man with a case of beer to rescue it each time his favorite foot squab hit the street. *"Can you imagine that?"*

"Yes, dear. I can imagine that."

"The Currie boys?" He grumbled some more, fascinated with the *tabloidal bizarrie* of the article, but unhappy with the account's inaccuracy.

Mary nodded absently, although absorbing everything he said, for she had a closer tie to the boys than he. She had known them personally. She had known their mother, as well. And she worried about them, *especially Eddie*, the younger one, now that Mother Currie was gone.

"But one thing you *can* rely on...," he began again, then trailed off, lost in thought, the image of an aging professor with too many details on his mind, too many paths to follow.

Mary smiled her *knowing* smile, while her husband's nose stuck close to the article, his reading lamp shadowing the whiskered creases of his neck, *like dried up river beds on Mars*, she would tease, the tinsel of his thinning hair, his spectacles hanging from his nose and which he only reluctantly wore because of the *really fine print* they're using now days, he would complain as if discounting his age, a curious reminder for her of *her own father—but she'd never tell Owen that*.

"What was that, dear?"

"*What?*"

"You know, '*...that you can rely on,*'" she reminded him.

"Oh, yeah, *their mother*. You know what an angel she was."

Mary knew.

"She didn't raise any common thieves," he insisted.

Mary knew *that*, too.

"And she didn't bring up murderers, for dang sure, like this high-rise writer seems to think," he poked at the paper, his eyes squinted narrow, his forehead furrowed with lines of thought. "Where do you suppose those *news* guys get their information from? Huh? Where do they come from with their *news* stories? Those *Tribune* guys," he harrumphed, slouching deeper into his chair.

"I wouldn't know, dear," she smiled.

"How could any one-of-'em know what went on up there with them boys, and how rough it is up there? *How isolated it is?*" he appealed as if *he* had known them all their lives, as if *he* had known Mother Currie, and as if *he* had been their supporter for as long as his wife had. "You think any of *them* lived up there where the Currie family grew up?"

"No, I don't suppose they did."

"Up on Currie Island?

"Yes, dear. 'Currie Island'"

"Why, hell, they'd get lost in a minute. I'll bet there's not ten people in the whole city who've even *seen* that spot," he rambled and grumbled along. "I'll bet no one around here could even *find* Currie Island, or Kettle Falls, or Big Timber, or any of them places...," he trailed off again.

Wondering who would be the *first one* to '...get lost', Mary nodded audibly over some last-minute adjustments to the waterproof boxes and assorted suitcases and handbags she was packing, even as she checked off items against a master list prepared weeks ago; and although accustomed to fending off her husband's editorial complaints, an evening ritual for her, this time she would agree, for the back-page headlines describing the Currie brothers as *armed and dangerous* was a waste of words, a waste of time. Except for their necessary fishing and hunting, they'd never harmed an innocent being in their lives. Whoever wrote the piece didn't understand the boys...their way of life. *For certain, the two were reclusive.* Few outsiders could claim to even *know* them. And *sure*, they were gullible and backwoods-like. *But not dangerous.* And hardly dishonest. She recalled the family had been close-knit; and she remembered the brothers as generous and as unassuming as were their parents, and deserving of a kinder bargain than the editorial allowed.

"It's too bad she didn't take us up on the Biscayne building last summer," Owen wandered.

"I suppose so. *We offered.* But you know that *that* building was—"

"Tore down for a parking lot," he grumbled. "The one Bill Qualley owned."

"Yes...your realtor friend; besides, that place was—"

"For the Medical Arts building."

"*I know*, but—"

"For their parking lot. We could have been neighbors."

"Yes, dear. But *not Mrs. Currie.*" She shook her head, forcing her brown eyes wide as Owen *finally* glanced up, her compelling *no way* look, for Mrs. Currie was no more a city dweller than were her sons.

Financially sensible, the building was an older duplex with income potential, instead of their imprudent purchase on Big Timber. But...*their survival in the cities?* She doubted they'd ever been so far south, grimacing at the thought of Eddie, with his patched-up bibs and rolled-up cuffs walking city streets. How could he *ever* tolerate city life? *Neither* drove a car, and *neither* understood public transportation; and *what would those wilderness boys do without their mother to guide them*, although Nels was better equipped.

"It says here they're *still* wanted for questioning—*I thought they dropped that silly notion*—for that missing attorney business some time back. You remember the one?" He raised his nose, but his eyes remained behind, captured by the writer's penchant for misinformation.

"I remember."

"That young fella out of Saint Paul? A single guy, wasn't he?"

"I believe so."

"Imagine…a green kid like that up there, and…," he drifted again.

"*'And'?*"

"And with all the trouble they were having up there? *Imagine that?*"

"'Imagine that,'" she smiled.

"That's as bad as them boys coming down *here* to live. *What in the world would they do in the cities?*" another wandering judgment.

And Mary smiled.

Then he repeated, "It says here how law officers found some of that ransom cash—*remember that ransom note they found?*—in a bait shop the boys bought. That place on Big Timber that old Bill Lawman owned."

Mary knew Big Timber.

"You remember Big Timber? How do you s'pose marked money found its way there—*if it wasn't them boys that hid it?*" a sarcastic dismissal, as he settled into an old tavern tune called Whiskey Bill:

Down the hill with gun in hand
Came Whisky Bill, came Whisky Bill,
Just looking for a place to land, came Whisky Bill.
The sheriff, he up and found his stride—
Bill soled and shoed him down the slide—
Oh how is it over the great divide of Whisky Bill?

While quietly rehearsing his hit-and-miss version, Owen fell to rummaging through the Tribune's mid-section to the sports pages, his eyes catching on the all-important *Wednesday Baseball Summary*. With his club on *another* winning streak this past stand, there were few things more important to him than weekend action at the dome where he could heckle the coach from his reserved seat along the third base line while eating cold hot dogs and drinking warm beer from a paper cup, a regular party atmosphere he was addicted to.

But he knew the call to *play ball* must wait because Uncle Ted Snelling, his woodsman brother-in-law, had *again* invited the family to his Kabetogema Narrows lake cabin, their annual retreat to the *wilds* of the North Country. Ordinarily their trip was an August berry-picking or a June walleye-fishing excursion on the sparsely populated Canadian border in what is now Voyageurs National Park. They'd headed up every spring or summer for the past eight years, and had always looked forward to their visits with Uncle Ted and their stops to see friends along the way.

But this summer promised to be different.

This summer, in addition to their traditional visit, Ted's invitation included a special request for Owen to stand radio watch for him while he was away on business in Saint Paul.

For years, even before he lost his Jenny, Ted maintained a park service navigation beacon and radio link on remote *Rocky Point*, his home on a cliff overlooking the Kabetogema narrows. Destined to be owned by the park service when he'd *eventually* leave it behind, his cabin was located above the mouth of Ash River, a landmark channel opening to a string of Minnesota boundary water lakes. His south shore location allowed him to closely observe the narrows, *a sometimes dangerous stretch of water*. His observations were then followed by an evening radio summary along with reports made by *other* civilian coast watchers, usually old-timers donating their services. Despite recent *technologies*, including satellite tracking and mapping devices that many adventurers had adopted, the weather was always unpredictable and potentially dangerous, so a wary coastline watch, *especially evenings*, was essential in Ted's world. Although an informal, voluntary patrol, Ted insisted it not be interrupted: shutting down was *no option* for Uncle Ted Snelling; so Owen agreed to substitute for him while he was away.

Substituting for Ted in a timely manner could have been a problem this year, for Owen couldn't simply take leave of his job whenever he pleased, *especially during audit time*. But Ted's unexpected business obligations and the Peterson's vacation schedule were a fortunate fit. The kids were unhappy with the arrangements because their paths would have to cross. With no way to avoid it, *each would be leaving on the same day, but in opposite directions:* the Petersons would be traveling north while Ted headed south—*on the same highway.* So *this* year, they'd not get to see each other until *after* Ted's return from the cities, and only *after* they'd settled in on the lake for a few days.

At least, those were the arrangements.

Sure, they would arrive to an empty cabin, and the kids would miss their uncle's familiar shout-and-wave, his invariable, "What took you city folks so long?" and, "You know how the weather can turn on a dime up here," he would repeat, striding down to his floating dock to greet them, with *Puck*, his black Lab companion leading the way. So practiced was he at traversing the suspended walkway that he hardly held on, *even in the wind;* and the kids marveled at this…*with the images and the memories and the stories all part of a ritual they anticipated and talked about each year.*

Those were the intentions this summer, *the crossing of paths.* The *unpopular* plans. *And the complaints,* as well. But those were plans the family was forced to deal with.

Little had changed with the arrangements—*until a day ago* when Owen's manager reported company audits ahead of schedule, with all accountant to be given extra time off. For the family this meant leaving a day earlier, *on Thursday;* so they could see Ted before he left, after all!

The kids were excited about this change of fortune, but without mail service at the cabin, and with no way to phone him, they elected to forego any relayed radio message from the landing and to surprise their woodsman uncle in the old-fashioned way by simply *showing up* on his doorstep, a common practice years ago. *Wouldn't that be great?* Perhaps *they* could even take him to the bus at Walker's Landing *themselves* on Friday.

Ted was the first of three Snelling children and had been closer to his oldest sister, *to Nancy,* than Mary was. Mary was much younger, her parents never lacking for a babysitter with Ted and Nancy nearby. But with Ted's double tragedy, the first—*Nancy's death*—ten years ago, things declined dramatically for him. Fortunes changed for his little sister, as well. When Nancy and her husband perished on a rain-slick highway north of the mining town of Virginia where the sawmill was located, Mary found herself within her new role as Ted's *oldest* sister, and now his *only* sister and confidant, *his only family.* Despite miles of wilderness between them, each became a part of the other's mind, the other's world.

But Ted's world would further collapse when his wife drowned in a hotly debated boating *mishap*. Closure was elusive because the accident was presumed by some, *including her brother,* to be more than a mere *accident.* With the mystery of that five-year-old tragedy derailing him for a second time, the Petersons found themselves among the few people with whom Ted felt comfortable, and with whom he could freely communicate.

Harboring no ill-will, blaming no one for the loss of either his wife or his sister, Ted remained trusting-enough of others, albeit isolated and sad, even disagreeable at times; but for those who knew him, his occasional moods were a *gruff-and-grumble* act that hid a kind and innocent soul.

Ted was no recluse. But since Jenny's death, he'd turned so introverted that when he wrote to report his *board meeting*, Mary was skeptical. *An emergency meeting? For his pulpwood operation?* She knew better than that. *There was nothing emergency about a pile of logs.* His offices *were* in the cities; but suspecting a diversion, Mary concluded that a recurrent, but *closely-held* health problem was the *real* emergency, and not a board meeting at all.

Mary was right about a diversion, for their rapport was a point of pride, a connection privy to few. But despite their understanding, *she failed to anticipate that it was neither his furtive illness nor his business obligations that would draw him away this summer.*

"Are the kids packed?" Owen brightened; but his real question was: *do you have all the bags packed yet?*

The Currie incident set aside, Owen's nose remained stuck between the lines of his *Sport Clips* and the latest *Plays of the Day*, while Dusty, their yellow spaniel, rejoined them by swishing his tail from side-to-side, his black eyes intense, the flurry of activity guaranteeing that something important was going on, and he wasn't about to miss out.

"Since this morning. They're excited. They can't wait," Mary smiled at her husband's inability to part himself from his sports pages. For certain, *Keith* couldn't wait. *He'd been ready all week.* But Mary knew that Jeremy was fast approaching her *stay-at-home* age, while the rest of the family went on vacation. Her older cousin from North Dakota made the trip to Berry Falls by herself each summer to stay with her grandmother—*and to see her boyfriend*—so that *must* have crossed her mind.

"O.K., dear, and bug repellant. Be sure you pack good bug repellant," he added absently while digesting the latest box scores and picks of the week. "And rain gear," he added, "for the mosquitoes," he trailed off.

"It's packed," she smiled, wondering where the aging professor's mind was headed.

"Remember the mosquitoes and the deer flies, and berry buckets. Plenty of berry buckets?"

"We'll have four of them."

"Ted doesn't keep any around, you know. He's got *no place to store them*, he says," his eyes glued to the paper, his face etched in baseball thought. "He figures *if they want to bite, let 'em bite.*"

"Jeremy's got them in the car," she giggled, realizing the uselessness of berry buckets in late June. For lack of boat space, they'd likely get left at the landing, anyway. By now, Gus Walkinen, the dock owner where Ted's spare boat was kept, had dozens of them under his back steps. Gus was a kind old man who'd become Keith and Jeremy's surrogate grandfather.

"And matches. My matchbox, Mary, and white gas and berry buckets; and don't forget jackets," he went on listing his disorganized string of *essentials* while continuing to pore over his column.

Mary was relieved. Recalling Owen's athletic family, she appreciated the *revitalization* the north woods provided each year. His brothers were active: one was a teacher and coach in Wyoming while another was a ranch-hand in the mountains near Beauty Lake, a picturesque pond on the Montana side. She remembered a trip across Bear Tooth Pass to visit him one summer where he worked on the Montana border at a *greenhorn* ranch. But to her husband's dismay, *everyone rode horse*. Owen was so uncomfortable in the saddle that summer that he stayed behind or rode a four-wheeler to keep up with the rest; and trout fishing with the group was out of the question. Growing up, he was active; but her transplanted city boy chose *accounting*, a sedentary switch for the once-robust Peterson clansman.

"All we need is lantern gas and some groceries," she replied, weaning her baseball critic from his column. "And we can get all *that* at the landing," she arose from re-arranging a suitcase. "Besides, you know how Ted is. *He'd never run short."* Mary knew that *running short* was unlikely because her brother was known to burn a candle—*or nothing at all*—rather than precious lantern fuel. But I'll be sure that match box is in your canvas jacket pocket—"

"My *fishing* jacket."

"Your *'fishing* jacket,'" she repeated with mock importance, appearing like a sweetly perfumed jack-in-the-box from behind the newspaper in which her husband was lost, "because you never know."

Peeking over the paper, she smiled at her spectacled, double-chinned baseball fan. Pretty, dark-haired, and slight, and with a turned-up nose that Owen teasingly compared to the neighbor's poodle, Mary's sparkling demeanor sharply contrasted her once-agile basketball star's sedentary workstyle. Always the outdoorswoman, Mary's heritage sprung from deep within the lakes and forests and the lore of the country for which they were headed, while her husband, a graying, slightly overweight armchair critic and incurable city dweller, struggled to understand her attraction for the north land, the monotony of endless lakes and trees, the claustrophobic tunneling of highways cut through dense forests, the insufferable summertime insects, and the constant threat of getting lost like tourists on the wrong end of Hennepin Avenue. He slowly learned to appreciate her *peace* in a country unpolluted by streams of commuters and street noises and mile-high office buildings. But it had taken time, his appreciation *still* influenced by the allure of baseball crowds and by the fast-paced existence only a *city boy* could understand.

Looking up, Owen grinned back. Reading her thoughts, he knew that if things were different, she would be happy to change plans and head for the ball park this week-end.

"An early start, Mary? Are the kids asleep?" he finally laid his newspaper aside.

She nodded demurely, "An hour ago, but it wasn't easy."

Chapter 2

The trip from the hub of Minnesota to the heart of the North Woods started early, wet, and dreary; but the cold rain settling in overnight wasn't the Petersons' main concern, rather it was in reaching the Ash River docks before dark, because the last leg of their journey was by boat, ten miles of open water and a final push through the shallows of Sullivan Bay that would take an hour. Although they left with plenty of time for rest and lunch breaks, flirting with daylight was unwise in the wild. Ted had often warned them against such imprudences, especially farther north where people were few, where boat traffic was light, and where chances of prompt discovery in the event of an accident were slim.

In the early years, access to Ted's *island*, the point of the nameless peninsula on which he lived, was possible only by water or sled. Aside from logging trails or pulpwood grades, the region's few roads made overland travel difficult. Recently, heavy roads and trucks made some inroads; but prior to the war years, the only wheeled transport for loggers was the Hoist Bay rail link joining the deep port on Namakan to the mill's main line at Virginia. But even *that* closed down when the snow got heavy and logging had to wait until spring.

Until recently, much of the area was only roughly sketched, *if mapped at all,* by the Indians and lumberjacks of old. But even on modern charts, most ranges, hilltops, and prominences *still* bear no names.

For those who'd settled the country into the new century, supplies had been boated in, the heaviest delayed until mid-winter, perhaps retrieved by motor sled or sleigh-and-team. Snowshoes and canoes had been common fare for everyone, especially the old-timers or the solitary hunter or ranger, or for the depression-era trapper who'd spurned the conveniences of motorized travel.

Accounts of those frontiersmen varied, some more myth than others; but one story passed about was more than legend: it was of a Dakota youth named Joe who, when he turned eighteen, watched his father die of gall bladder infection during the days when infections were death knells; so amidst the Depression, Joe was obliged to support his mother and younger brothers. Jobs were scarce—*that was no legend*—and the war and FDR hadn't arrived yet; so after struggling to make a living as a farm worker and carpenter's helper while shooting jackrabbits for food with surplus military rounds, he packed his gear and bummed the rails east and north, landing employment at Ed and Linda Foster's trading post along Pelican River in Minnesota's North Woods where a little of *everything* could be bought, bartered, or sold for gold.

Ed's brother-in-law, the local magistrate, closed his eyes to the illegal pelts Ed took from the Indians then passed on to a Canadian trader named Rene Beaudoin (who provided the judge with a kickback for his assistance). This activity was not lost on Joe who understood the unreasonableness of game laws written by out-of-touch politicians unfamiliar with snowshoes or trapper shacks or water sets cut into banks of beaver ponds.

Joe did well as a handyman at Foster's, soon catching the attention of Linda's attractive sister, Alice Jarvenin, also employed at the post, as well as looks from Judge Loomis's slow-to-go daughter, three years Joe's senior, who aspired to a claim on him because of the favors her father provided his employer, this competition making Joe's presence at the store so stressful that he felt compelled to move out of the *visitors' cabin* that he'd been living in nearby the river.

Although Ed understood Joe's dilemma, for they were friends by now, he advised keeping his day job; but with female problems looming, and with the lure of better money in the intangible *out there,* Joe switched to timbering in the vastness of Saint Louis County where he loaded logs onto railroad flatcars at the deep port on Namakan's Lake's Hoist Bay. But that industry had been waning since the early twenties. So as boundary waters froze over,

Joe realized that trapping (with Ed and Lawyer Loomis's assistance) was more profitable than timber; and manning Forest Service fire towers was more peaceful than harvesting white pine for the Virginia sawmill; and in spite of Ed's red-headed sister-in-law standing by with her hopes on hold (Joe secretly saw Alice on occasion, and she would drive to the station when he needed supplies or to transport his pelts), the woods beat working at the store where he risked a face-off with the judge by having to deny his homely offspring.

Without formal education, Joe taught himself mathematics while passing winter evenings in his trapper shack, with a wood fire in a crude-built fireplace and a kerosene lantern alongside, and he would drink *trapper* coffee, or sweet-smelling pine needle tea when coffee ran short and chew on boiled beaver tail when flour ran low; and when math got monotonous, he would read The Histories of Civilizations and the E. Haldeman-Julius *Little Blue Books* classics: Faust, DeMauppasant, Hugo, Saki, and William Shakespeare. Evenings were lonely-cold and quiet; but they were peaceful to the brink of religious as snow would fall in diamond-studded flakes, when the ground wind was held trapped and tamed through sieves of pine and poplar, and the temperature fought its way to even.

Before sunrise, wearing snowshoes made of twisted deer hide and white ash frames fitted over oil-sealed packs, and with his coyote-trimmed, goose down parka aback, Joe would set out with his rifle in hand and knapsacks laden with traps, chains, shovel, waxed paper, bait, scent, carcass carriers, and flour and coffee;

and he would retrieve and revive water sets for mink and beaver until darkness shut him down.

His line shacks which he used if unable to return to his cabin, were located near springs and streams feeding Ash River, some little more than lean-to shelters, while others were dirt-floored, single room structures with a fireplace and trapping gear along one wall, and a split-log cot on the other.

While in the woods, his was a lonely existence. His only contact with *community* were his weekly canoe runs down the river where Sullivan Bay narrows to some docks and trading spots near the Ash River Station; while fifty miles south at Berry Falls was Foster's Trading Post where his young lady friend worked and waited for his call.

When waterways were open and lines were active, he might harvest more than legal. But *no apologies,* he learned from Ed and the judge who promoted the practice, because during tough times, survival and regulations often collide, the two mutually meaningless, just as it was with Prohibition when liquor laws were impulsively pushed by special interests ignorant of organized crime and collateral consequences.

So began the *good verses good* symbiosis when the local warden, young and capable, met Joe at the post and was his *cohort* everywhere but in the woods. When they encountered each other at work, Bill would remind his trapper friend about the game regulations he knew were being manipulated under his nose, *even by the judge,* and about his own obligation to uphold the law; and they would argue—*even agree over a beer*—about what was fair and what was right.

One evening when Bill was *fishing* a dam for a cable-and-weight he'd discovered (he swore he didn't know the beaver set was Joe's), he slipped on spillway ice, fell in, and caught his pack on a stick of beaver cut. Secretly, Joe was watching and saved his friend from drowning. He even re-entered the water to retrieve the warden's rifle, then pulled the trap himself to prove it trailed a legal slide and weights.

Two months later, Bill ran across Joe and Alice returning from the Ranger Station. While changing a tire on the highway, Joe had to remove pelts from under the back seat of her Chevrolet to reach the jack and stand stored there. Bill could have fined him because the season was over and Joe's possessions were illegal. But he concluded that his friend had no way to transport the pelts in proper parcels.

Each with a job to do, each with skills honed to trip the other, they shared a mutual respect that lasted until the war invaded their lives. By then, Joe had given up trapping and lumbering to be a forest ranger. Before leaving for boot camp, Bill was Joe's best man when he married Alice at International Falls. They did their best to stay in touch; but Bill, an infantry officer, was killed in Africa two years later, while Joe survived. Upon his return from Italy, he and Alice settled in the Dakotas; and from there they vacationed in Minnesota with their family for years to come.

The ruggedness of the old days had lost its edge, the country grown seductively tamer and electronically accessible; and even since Ted and Mary were children, modern mapping and mechanization had taken over. But memories of the tough old men like Bill and Joe remained sharp, rugged and romanticized. On occasion, a group would gather before the evening fire at Klostermans, or they might crowd the oak table in the back room of Walkers Landing where tales were embellished for the young and for the young at heart; and Keith would hear of the hunter or trapper like Joe (stories and characters would change with the teller) getting weathered in by "…a howling blizzard come roaring in from out of the north…," or by the "…takin' on a pack of silver wolves so hungry your neck hair stood on end." Or the time half the folks in the county had been summoned to search for a five-year-old who'd strayed from the family camp and had gotten lost.

Perhaps Keith was hiking or trap-checking through this dreamscape of jack pine and timber wolves, perhaps himself pursued by an angry mother-bear he happened upon while working his string of snow sets from shack-to-shack, maybe even sprinting for safety, as he awoke with a start:

"Are we there yet?" Yawning, he looked about, rubbing his sleep-heavy eyes. "Is it still raining?" he wondered, scratching himself most *inappropriately* for his sister to behold. For a twelve-year-old, Keith knew the route well, having traveled it every year for as long for as *he* could remember. *And that was a long time*, he would argue. But the blue-eyed, blond-haired adventurer had been napping since their Crescent Falls lunch stop an hour-and-a-half earlier, a reprieve for Jeremy from his wide-grinned bantering and teasing. The two could get along, but not *"...cooped up for hours with him...,"* she would complain.

"We've another hour to the docks," his mother replied as Keith began picking out familiar points along the way, even in the rain.

"Did we eat yet?" more alertly, he peered through rain-streaked windows at one of the numerous lakes and ponds dotting northern Minnesota. Dusty's ears perked at the prospect of dinner, while an exasperated, "Oh-h-h..." came from his sister, like steam from a laundry vent.

"That's all he ever thinks about, unless he's sleeping," Jeremy scowled, firmly closing her book and throwing it on the seat beside her—on *her* side of the invisible curtain separating his world from hers, her solitude ruined. *Some trip this was going to be.*

"Look at the black ducks, dad...on the water down there," he interrupted his sister's thoughts.

"Those aren't ducks. They're loons," his father replied. "And that's Pelican Lake," he added. While Keith was sleeping—*and just now waking up*—they were driving their way through the resort community of Berry Falls where many motels and chalets were built along the shoreline of Pelican Lake. They might have stopped at a rest area earlier on, for Jeremy was a poor traveler; but she insisted, *at all cost,* that he not be awakened. "Loons are like ducks, but tough and fishy. You wouldn't want to eat 'em."

"*Loons,*" Keith grinned. *This was going to be a fun trip.*

"We decided to wait until Klostermans," his mother smiled, privately deciding that Jeremy was too harsh with her brother, maybe a little selfish, all-the-same realizing Keith could handle himself. "Your Uncle Neal might have a surprise in store, and Aunt Becky knows we're coming. She'll have something special ready, maybe one of her Southern dishes everyone likes."

"Yeah, and maybe blueberry turnovers."

"Maybe so."

This was acceptable, for Aunt Becky was an *awesome* cook; and Klostermans was a fun place, an old-fashioned waterfront restaurant with a musty, rustic, pine-finished tone, and with the unmistakable odor of ripe blueberries and parched wild rice permeating the air like in an old trading post that had seen its share of seasons. Many dated deer trophies and black-bear hides and a timber-wolf-of-old lined its log-cabin-styled walls, as well as ancient pictures and traps and pelts and assorted backwoods gear accumulated over the years. There was even a North American bald eagle behind glass (this one was mounted and registered during the days when it was still legal to possess them) in an upper back-corner of the restaurant's dining room. The shores and docks of Ash River, where Uncle Neal had a line of rental boats and canoes of his own, was Keith's most favorite place this side of Uncle Ted's cabin (if you didn't count the Diamond Jack Arcade at the shopping mall). On their return from Ted's, staying over a day or two was a real possibility. They had plenty of room, Keith knew, and Uncle Neal might let him run the little ten-footer by himself, he thought, as he debated residency on the river, and maybe even a job at one of the local tackle shops, or at the Big Dipper ice cream store where they had a game room in back.

"But if you're hungry, there's some sandwiches in the cooler."

"Sure, if Jeremy didn't eat 'em all already," he rummaged about for a container of chocolate chip cookies that he knew were packed because his mother made them last night after he went to bed.

Another exasperated, "Oh-h-h", along with a *"Mother, does he have to? And why can't he comb his hair. Look at that mess. It's all matted down from sleeping half the day."*

Aside from the rain and bits of sibling friction, the trip was going smoothly, with light traffic since mid-morning, since crossing the imaginary boundary separating northern Minnesota from its more populated south. But just outside a small lake community within the Iron Range, they came across a series of temporary *reduced speed* signs set up along the road, and northbound vehicles began to slow down, a line-up developing in the rain. This might be expected in the cities with their constant roadwork and stop-and-go commuters and snarled interchanges, but to happen so far north was unusual.

Ted told the story of a bridge washing out north of Berry Falls one spring when it rained so heavy along Pelican River, *the way he related it*, that the rice fields were carried away with the flood. They weren't carried away at all; but he made his point that, in lake country, driving one's way around that sort of trouble, around bridge washouts and flooded and damaged roads, without heavy equipment on hand, was often impossible because right-of-ways were frequently built high and over swampy ground, while back roads remained sparsely constructed, dead-end and unreliable, and not at all typical of the mile-apart Land Ordinance section lines of 1785 that were common on the plains.

"What do you suppose?" Mary wondered. "Was there an accident up there? *Do you think anyone got hurt?*"

Owen shrugged, "I hope not."

"Could it be highway work?" she tried again.

"I don't expect so. Not in this soup. They'd never get anything done," he peered past the hypnotic *back-and-forth* of the wiper blades at pockets of water in the ditches and low places, the country reminiscent of reservation swamplands where he had seen wild rice harvested with canoes and four-foot-long clubs that were tapered at the working end. He remembered how native harvesters on Nett Lake would slide their canoes in patterned swaths through the rice marshes—*he watched them for an hour one day*—then recalled how *one* harvester would stand in the back of the craft with a fifteen-foot pole to guide them along, while *another* would bend the reeds over their floating holds while beating the rice into the canoe with his pair of clubs, *back and forth* they would go, slipping through the rice paddies…*back and forth the windshield wipers paced.* Working in pairs within each canoe, one would pole while the other would work the crop. But as they made their way through the shallow-water fields, they would leave plenty of seed behind for the following year's harvest. "But those warning signs must mean *something*," he continued, as they slipped on through the rain.

Presently, traffic slowed some more. Then it crawled. *And then it stopped completely.* Several hundred feet ahead, two white patrol cars could be seen parked askew with amber lights flashing, along with uniformed men in black rain gear taking charge. It was all so official, so stark and so surreal, with cars and trucks lined up and travelers being scrutinized by officers working with cold efficiency from vehicle to waiting vehicle. It was obvious they were searching for something *or someone.*

"Was there an accident?" Keith asked over his shoulder as he chomped on a cookie while kneeling on Jeremy's pillow which she'd allowed to escape her reach, even as he dropped crumbs on the seat alongside.

"Oh, for...*didn't mom already ask that?*" she started, snatching the pillow out from under him, all to Keith's delight.

"I don't know. It could be. For sure there's a roadblock," his father explained, realizing that with the wet weather and the scarcity of back roads in these marshes, this was an ideal spot for a highway check, for *whatever* reason.

"Oh, my. How long will *this* take?" Mary's fears were in arriving at the docks too late for a visit with the Klostermans before having to depart for her brother's cabin, or *worse yet,* being forced to unload their boat in the dark once they arrived up there—*or even in the rain. And what if it was windy or storming?* she worried some more, a string of *what ifs* invading her mind. Ted had often warned them about allowing adequate travel time so far north, reminding them that his navigation beacon, or the *light of the blue moon,* as he put it, were poor substitutes for daylight on the open water, while repeating details of how she an Owen were forced to stay overnight with the kids at Klostermans two springs ago when it

sleeted so badly they couldn't see to navigate, the same season they had snow on the ground in the middle of June.

And Owen understood his wife's concern as she recalled that less-than-memorable *one cloudy evening* incident when he and Keith had been out fishing too late and too far from the cabin and had to rely on that beacon to make it *home* again. With no radio in the boat, Owen had no desire to repeat the ordeal. It had been a grand adventure for Keith, churning through the dark without lights and the wind up and nothing to guide on but that flashing blue signal. In fact, the danger may have been overblown that evening, with Ted having a judicious chuckle over it because the boys hadn't gone very far—*and they caught no fish;* but the chance of getting lost or of running into a half-submerged rock or floating debris was real-enough for little-tested city-dwellers to avoid risking again.

"Are they looking for someone?" A serious tone invaded Keith's fun time, his nose pushed like a mushroom against the window, fogging it over.

"I don't know. It could be," his father repeated, even as Jeremy turned serious, her brown eyes darting from her father's face to the scene outside and back again; and, for a change, no one knew any more than what her brother knew.

After eventually being questioned by two brusque patrolmen, each peering like expressionless aliens through half-opened windows with the rain dripping off their hooded gear, and over Dusty's loud protests, they were waved off by a third.

Jeremy was the first to ask, "What did they say, Dad? *What did they want?* I couldn't hear what they were saying with Dusty barking in my ear," she scowled at the little dog which seemed to share Keith's grin.

"Nothing. There's *nothing* to worry about. They just wanted to know where we're going, honey, and if mother and I recognized the men in the pictures they had. I'm sure they could see we're on vacation," he smiled stiffly, considering their line of sealed luggage and the waterproof bags tied atop the van.

"What men? Who are they looking for? Are they criminals or something?" Keith turned from the window, a concerned look clouding his face, a serious tone invading his fun time.

"Oh, for…," Jeremy complained again under her breath, as if *she* knew something her brother didn't know—*but should have*.

"We don't know, son," his mother allowed. "They don't explain things like that. I imagine that *whoever* it is, they'll be in the news tomorrow. You can listen for it on your uncle's radio."

Mary concealed her apprehensions not only over what she knew of her brother's kinship with the young men the officers were searching for, but that she and Owen *also* knew them, *that she had known them practically all their lives,* although neither had seen or spoken to the pair in years; and she struggled over the prospect of turning them in if the opportunity was forced on them.

"I'm just glad they didn't take too long," she glanced at her husband who pretended to concentrate on the road, both holding in private torment over their denial of *ever* associating with Nels and Eddie Currie and over their conviction that the brothers were incapable of doing anything wrong.

After another half hour of silence, with each family member lost in his own reflections, the Petersons finally came to a roadway rest area near the long-awaited sign signaling the end of their Highway Fifty-Three drive north, and the start of the next leg of their journey to remote Kabetogema Lake:

ASH RIVER TRAIL
ONE MILE

More than a mere trail, or more than simply the *ranger station access road,* the roadway was originally constructed through marshland, sometimes over immense floating barges crisscrossing grown-over lakes and swamps in a time of hazardous and unpredictable travel. Of late, the Ash River Trail had been transformed into nine miles of modern highway lined with advertising signs and billboards inviting tourists and travelers to the cabins, campgrounds, and boating facilities strung out along lower Ash River, with visitors frequently making their reservations years in advance. These sights were rejuvenating in a *touristic* way. Affecting them all, even Jeremy revealed hints of reluctant anticipation as they passed the first of the gas-and-gift shops introducing them to a variety of establishments grown to become a small town, a striking contrast to the few stores and dock-houses Mary remembered as a girl. *Her* place in this *trap* had roots far deeper than the footings of billboards erected over the years, or of the dredged-out river channel that supported more wildlife than it did now. She was a part of the stories her father and grandfather had told of trap lines and fire towers, of her mother's recollections of trading with the Indians, of parching wild rice and picking blueberries, of her summer excursions with her mom and dad and brother and sister to Linda's cabin on the north shore of Kabetogema Lake, and of her own bitter-sweet memories of Linda Foster's trading post south of Berry Falls before it mysteriously burned to the ground.

The area's popularity had rapidly developed over recent years, that growth but a nitch in the wilderness they were about to enter. There was a line, albeit an imaginary one drawn a few miles upriver beyond which few unguided tourists crossed; getting lost or stranded on *those* waters, *especially at night*, was a reality no tenderfoot cared to chance.

Chapter 3

The Petersons were headed for the Park. *And what a grand park it is!* Within its boundaries hundreds of lakes fill glacial-carved rock basins, while four larger bodies called Rainy, Kabetogema, Namakan, and Sand Point protect Minnesota's northern border. Rainy is the largest, Sand Point the most easterly of the string. Hundreds of islands, bogs, bays, and rocky outcrops, named and unnamed, scatter throughout. Some of the shelves hide below the water line where deep-keeled boats might meet trouble, while others are large enough to live on. At one time the water was lower, but with modern dams and power stations, many outcrops were covered and shorelines changed, and old rice fields, especially on Namakan, were destroyed. At the center of this expanse on the Southern Canadian Shield lies the Kabetogema Peninsula, 75,000 acres of roadless hills, swamps, and beaver ponds, the whole of which heads for Hudson Bay. The area boasts some of the oldest landforms in the world, sprinkled throughout with a delicate layer of soil supporting a boreal ecosystem rivaling any in grandeur and variety.

Unlike today's *adventurers*, recent natives knew only the limitations of weather and natural boundaries, just as *their* ancestors did when roaming the shores of Lake Agassiz which covered much of northern Minnesota and eastern North Dakota. For a time, the Huron and Chippewa prevailed, then were displaced by the Dakota and Ojibwe, each leaving evidence of their unique cultures found in pictographs on the Basswood River, Agnes Lake, Lac La Croix, Kahshahpiwi Lake, and Fishdance. Contrasting today's stewards, these people lived in harmony with nature; they were the *real* stewards, the *real* caretakers.

Learning from them and bartering with them were the French Canadian *Voyageurs* who moved beaver and other hides between Montreal and the Canadian Northwest. These trailbreaker-traders, explorers in their own right, began plying the waters in pine-tarred, birch bark canoes three hundred years ago. Carrying guns, kettles, fabrics, and other goods to trade for furs, these hearty canoe men worked for companies interested in pelts for top hats, capes, and muffs popular in Europe until the 1850's. A typical season had some leaving their winter ports on Rainy Lake in mid May, usually reaching Grande Portage by late summer with their collections of furs, while others left Montreal loaded with food and trade goods to be exchanged for the furs at Grande Portage, both parties returning to their cold-weather ports before the winter freeze. Their routine became so established that the

1783 treaty ending the American Revolution specified that the Canadian-American boundary should follow their customary route between Lake Superior and Lake of the Woods.

With new roads and railroads and advanced water transport, adventurers and investors took interest in the area; and in 1893, when prospectors discovered gold on Little America Island, news spread and people traveled by rail from Duluth to Vermillion Lake, then by wagon and waterway to Rainy Lake where the gold was found. But the rush was brief. There were financial and production problems, and isolation and extreme living conditions. With the added lure of the Klondike, the mines were abandoned, and by 1910 most miners were gone.

But *real* change came with loggers and lumbermen cutting millions of white and red pine and spruce and fir. Unlike Uncle Ted's pulpwood operation where chainsaws are the tools of trade, old-timers used two-man handsaws and axes, and horse and sleigh, and winch and crane, as they cut and hauled virgin timber to the waterways of the border lakes. Forty lumber camps operated in the park at the peak of logging between 1907 and 1929, with the Virginia and Rainy Lake lumber company claiming title as primary harvester. They built a railroad spur into Hoist Bay on Namakan Lake from where they hauled logs onto flatcars for transport to the largest white pine sawmill in the world at Virginia. But by 1920 these companies had so devastated the land that the once abundant virgin timber was gone forever.

Commercial fishing for sturgeon and the caviar it produced, along with walleye, pike, and whitefish began with the gold rush, reaching its peak about 1910 when opposition to this industry forced broad regulations. With the decline of commercial fishing, resort owners and entrepreneurs welcomed sporting anglers and tourists, with real tourism escalating with the completion of highway 53 in 1922, the very highway on which the Petersons were traveling.

Between 1920 and 1940, resorts and summer homes appeared all along the lakeshores. Some cabins like Uncle Ted's and Aunt Linda Foster's and the Currie's and the Halsinen's were year-rounders, but most were not. And while some were built on privately owned property on Kabetogema's southern side, *what little private property there was*, the park service bought up the greater share and later recalled their long term leases, as well.

Wildlife abounds in number and diversity in the park. These include black bear, the smallest and the most abundant in North America, and the only bear in Minnesota. There are moose, elk, and deer, along with beaver, muskrat, weasel, and the snowshoe hare; while loons, ospreys, ducks and geese, the regal northern bald eagle, and songbirds of endless size and song fill the air. But the park is also central to the only region in the continental United States where the eastern timber wolf is a natural survivor. Nothing so symbolizes the park's primitivism as the presence of these shy and secretive animals which are so few in number that visitors seldom see them. Living in small packs and covering perhaps forty miles in a night's hunt, timber wolves may kill large animals for food, but more frequently feed upon beaver. Old-timers tried their hand at trapping wolves in addition to the beaver they preyed upon, but that activity was made illegal many years ago. Now, on a moonlit night, and if you listen very closely, you might hear the lonesome and ancient howl of the lobo while sitting around a campfire or while drifting off to sleep.

Chapter 4

"That's the way!" Keith pointed to the crossroads leading to Klostermans Bar and Café. The rain having abated, his spirits were soaring, and he was eager to get to the business of *checking out* the place. He hadn't been here in a year and *a lot* of things must have changed by now. "The next turn, Dad! You see it?" he gestured, *"You see it?"* He bounced around the back seat like a ping-pong ball while his sister glared at him even as she pressed purposely into *her* corner of the car. She wasn't about to get excited by anything her brother was interested in. *What if someone should find out?*

"I see it," his father grinned, *"I see it."* The roadblock incident was temporarily forgotten, the Currie boys backstaged for now. *This trip was for the kids,* Owen decided. It wasn't fair to worry them with personalities they had no connection to, with complications they didn't understand, or with reminiscences he and Mary were willing to forgo.

But as they approached *Corner Cross*, a stone marker on a path that led to a non-denominational cemetery no longer used because of its inconvenient location, and the supporting church closed down and replaced by a motel and strip mall, it was Mary who held to reminisce. It was with a feeling of foreboding as *the Cross* reminded her of *Cross in Hand* in Tess of the D'Urbervilles, "…the unholy stone whereon Tess was compelled by Alec…" to swear a strange oath; and Mary wondered if the strange oath, *the lie she told the patrolmen on the highway* would come back to haunt her. It wasn't like her to *unbend* the truth, an alien diversion in a land of purity, and…*she caught herself, a wistfully Victorian mood from wherein she forced herself back to reality.*

Unlike her husband, she had been a part of the docks, a part of the past; and she'd been a part of the people living here because *she* grew up here. The Klostermans and the Snellings were close back then. And Neal and his sister, too. Later, after Jenny Klosterman became Ted's wife, *stopping by* was more than a visit, for best friends had become family.

"Nope, it *just ain't right,* folks," Neal entered with a flourish a half-hour after the Petersons sat down for a late lunch. Still upset, he'd been at a *town meeting* up the road with neighborhood *governors* discussing public funding for a community boat ramp that threatened his business while the Petersons visited with his wife. *Governors* was a tag Neal pinned on local businessmen not owning riverfront property but who felt the cost of public access should be shared by everyone including dock owners; and this set him fuming. When he arrived, somewhat settled after his walk back, he offered to radio Ted to let him know they'd come a day early; but Mary declined, deciding to surprise her brother by simply dropping in on him, the way it was done before the days of dependable two-way radios. Neal and Becky thought it was a bad idea to *drop in* on Ted like that, but Mary persisted.

Becky Peterson—*Rebecca*, Neal would call her when stressed or pressed with importance matters—was a Delta Belle, a New Orleans lady, whose mother's maternal side was exiled from Acadia in 1755. Although a true Louisianan, she fell in love with the North Country—*with Neal*—while on a family fishing outing twenty years earlier, and refused to return home with them. Now the head cook, bookkeeper, and bottle-washer of their enterprise, she was so particular about Neal's spending that she threatened to fire him if she got a raise, a warning over which Neal would elevate his brows, saying, *"…and she's not kidding."* Often quoting Mark Twain's claim that "New Orleans food is as delicious as the less criminal forms of sin," she knew a good deal of the Creole and Cajun cuisine, the black iron one pots including Jambalaya, grillages, stews, and gumbos; and she routinely turned them out as part of her menu. Hers was an unusual and widely touted *carte du jour* on the river. Despite coming from backgrounds defying comparison, Neal and Becky were as inseparable as they were contentious.

Tossing his leather cap onto the hook of a birch coat-rack that ran in a continuous circumference about the room, Neal slid in alongside Owen at the corner booth of his knotty-pine-lined dock-side trophy room, while his wife re-set the table with homemade ice cream and blueberry turnovers fresh from the oven. Passing up desert (This was out of character for Keith), Jeremy and her brother elected to explore the docks while Mary and Owen got caught up on events—*on Currie events*. It was well after the noon rush, the restaurant no longer crowded except for a straggler-or-two; and it was safe to talk.

"Nope, it don't make no sense those boys ain't been caught," Neal shook his head. But more than the mordant dock owner, Neal was convinced that recent *observations* were connivery, that no one would see the brothers alive again. Without evidence, for *rumors were hardly evidence,* he realized that no one had seen them in months. "It's like they slipped off the edge," he motioned, "like when Jenny up and disappeared. No one's seen hide nor hair of her, neither."

"So you don't believe they're back." Mary *also* discounted the *sightings* stretching in imagination from a Hennepin nightclub to a sportsmen's bar at Cormorant Falls where they were *observed* playing pool with a motorcycle crew and their lady friends; except no one could *pin down* who'd done the *observing.*

"Nope. I sure don't, Mary," he darkened.

"Or that they'll *ever* come back," she quietly summarized. With Neal's concern laid bare, she knew he was convinced of the same fate that had befallen his sister five years earlier. She knew this *still* exacted a toll on him, for he and Jenny had been as one-of-mind as she and Ted were now. Unlike herself and her brother, Neal had no one else to help recall poignant family *facts*, insignificant to anyone else, but so important to him.

He shrugged, "We heard some of the ransom money showed up at that bait place they bought—*Lawman's old spot, ya know*—the one the old bachelor tried dumpin' before he left. Hell, for all it was worth, he should have burned the place down before movin' on. Even the park service don't want to buy it. *He should have known better.* He didn't get nothing for it, anyway," he grumped. "But nobody *I* know laid eyes on 'em," he pulled at his mustache, a silvery protrusion setting off his cobbled face. *"No doubt,* stuff's been missin' 'round here—*stuff's missin' all the time.* So suspicious folks (simple folks, I say) figure it's *gotta* be them. But if you want *suspicious*, I could name you some preachers an' politicians—*an' land men—ain't that right, Rebecca*—who's more *suspicious* than them Currie boys," an indictment of a real-estater floating about in his flashy tri-hull, out of place and useless.

"What *'stuff'*, Neal?" Mary remembered the two boys as harmless, honest, and likely nowhere near.

"Wa-a-l, someone made off with my squareback canoe last fall—*the one Victor Jarvenin gave me;* an' two weeks ago, Simon Genre's mercantile got broke into—*he never leaves cash around,* ya know, 'cause he never *could* get his back door to lock proper. An' I don't think he even knows what a safe is. So, was it flour an' coffee that got took?" he narrowed. "*Sure* it was. But that was only for show. Simon said there wasn't near enough missing for any turn in the woods. What-the-hell's a few pounds of flour gonna do? But *so what?* They don't need no supplies nohow, 'cause they *also* been seen *in the cities.* Them boys ain't been in no woods, *'cause they magically turned into city folks,"* he braved sarcasm.

Mary started then paused at his cynicism, the impossibility of young Eddie playing billiards in the smoke-filled back room of Chelsie's parlor, a ridiculous image conjured by people unfamiliar with his background or unappreciative of the brothers' passion for the wilderness.

"But you know what else they took? *Binoculars.* An' ice-cream bars. An' cigarettes, too. Fact is, *mostly* cigarettes," he thumped the table. "You ever know them boys to smoke? Why, *hell...,*" He sat back, his face a challenge; and no matter that Neal's words centered on *the boys,* Mary knew that *Jenny* had re-entered his mind; and she could tell by his furrowed forehead that Neal suspected a connection among his sister, the attorney, and the elusive Currie boys, an uncomfortable but logical conclusion.

Just then, Jeremy walked in through the river-side lobby, with Dusty panting close behind. Sporting muddy feet and dragging ears, with his tail swashing from side-to-side like a wet straw broom, the little dog had been on a long run.

"Who, Mom? *Those criminals?*"

A dog free-wheeling through the restaurant would have turned attention in the cities, or at least the head of the health inspector; but it was hardly noticed on the river.

"*Where's your brother,* young lady?" her mother flashed, the Currie incident fresh on her mind. *"He's not alone, is he?"* her worry reflecting their conversation's tenor, that he might have tumbled into the water someplace or gotten lost.

"Oh, he's O.K. He *was* looking at animal furs and deer heads in the other room," she screwed up her face, presenting her *sour* look like a young girl should. Anticipating her mother's concern, Jeremy's grimace was a carefully choreographed, in-front-of-the-mirror distraction, a purposeful change of direction, for Keith may have been outside, but he was *nowhere near the docks;* rather, he was where she left him *by himself* a quarter-mile away, *across the park service walk bridge and up the river,* spying on a pair of nesting ducks from the confines of a grass covered hut on Donavan Marsh.

While the older folks reminisced with coffee and tarts over old times and recent events, Jeremy and her brother were exploring their surroundings looking for new friends and fresh adventures; and not to be disappointed, a few doors upriver where the neighborhood dock joins a public ramp, they met a strange fellow a year or two older than Jeremy and slender to the point of emaciation. Tall, and dressed in rolled-up denims, sizes too large, and held together at the waist by a webbed belt, the young man had a head of curly-black locks that looked the crown of a shampooed poodle, blow-dried and pampered. This he topped with a threadbare tank cap of questionable origin which he routinely removed and used for everything from wiping his brow to slapping zebra-striped deer flies off dock posts. He was *cute enough,* but *shifty-eyed,* Jeremy thought, their new companion nevertheless friendly and full of improbable claims of kings' ransoms, secret hideouts, and powerful friends. He was chock-full of soaring tales and colorful Bounty-type stories that Keith eagerly absorbed while swearing to a lifetime of secrecy, as if Freddie had sailed to Ocracoke, himself. Removing his hat with a flourish, their audacious friend would point about and play the authority, their unofficial river guide. But he spoke nothing of friends or family or of growing up. Instead, as if a long-time resident (Jeremy knew he'd arrived last summer, that he was a trouble-maker in the past, and that he now stayed at the Walker House where the postmaster lived), he singled out spots and shops along the docks, telling how, "I know things..." about each, and how they figured into his fancifully vague plans for the area, the town's one-day *godfather*. Jeremy realized that even *she* knew more than he did about the river and the people living here. *Even her brother knew more*, but she politely allowed him his show. And Keith was so taken up with him that he hardly noticed any flaws at all.

Presently, following their companion's prattle and bravado, they crossed a suspended foot bridge spanning Ash River, and where a walk path wound them through a manicured but unfrequented park and picnic area adjoining a section of uninhabited woods. Then after crossing an obscure trail on the park's outskirts, they were led to a reed-infested lagoon locally called Donavan Marsh, named after the obscure *Earl of Donnovan—from the Isles,* locals claimed, although how true was never substantiated...

...Tall and handsome and with a bravado rivaling Keith and Jeremy's new friend, the *Earl*, an habitual liar—*a gold hunter*, despite having *never* been seen prospecting—was burdened by a string of debts run up by his alleged *daughter*, a woman he routinely argued with, and nearly as old as he. When she was kidnapped (some say, *absconded*) by *natives*, he'd promptly set out to *rescue* her. Days later, his hotel room was found empty *and unpaid*, neither he nor his *daughter* heard from again....

...A few yards away, as they approached the timber-drowned end of an over-bloomed lily pond, they discovered a pair of nesting Mallards which their friend, in an out-of-character gesture, admonished them not to frighten; and on one end of the marsh was hidden a crude lean-to contrivance of bark and sticks and faded binder-twine that Jeremy and her brother would have entirely missed if not nosed directly to it.

"C'mon, I'll show you something," he invited as they crawled, one-at-a-time, into his makeshift structure where, once inside, he uncovered an opening to an unobstructed view of the water. "Over there," he pointed proudly to his ducks, while shoving a brand-new pair of binoculars into Keith's hands.

As her brother peered between two stands of cattails and across blankets of lily pads, it occurred to Jeremy that they had not yet exchanged names; and only after she informed their *river guide* who they were and where her family was heading off to that evening did his *cavalierite'* break. In fact, he said little at all when he found out about Uncle Ted and their impending trip up the river this evening. And considering the bluster with which he entered their dockside adventure, his change of equanimity was significant. Suddenly reflective, he declared:

"I've got to go. You coming?"

Undaunted by this transformation, Jeremy agreed to return to the docks with him, but Keith refused with an, "it's not time yet." Reluctantly, and only because the path to Klostermans was easy to follow and that her brother had been this way before, did she allow him to remain, with a promise to come back soon, and to return the binoculars to where their friend had concealed them within a waterproof bag in the floor of his hideout.

"Who were you talking about just now?" Jeremy repeated, with all the concern a young girl *with something to hide* could muster.

"Those two the police were looking for—"

"*They're up here? Those crooks?*" She leaned forward on her very toes, her eyes widened in mock alarm, fooling nearly everyone with her *anticipation*.

"No, now don't you worry, dear," her aunt interjected, caught up by the act, even as Neal rolled *his* eyes, *not caught up at all*. "They're harmless. Just good old boys, you know," her Cajun accent a mixture of French and Southern drawl. "Those dear boys wouldn't hurt anyone." She patted Jeremy's arm, then pulled up a chair for her at the opened end of the booth.

Secretly, Jeremy resented the *Betty Crocker* supraconsolation because it made her feel *less-than-adult;* but it was with a guilty pause because she liked her Aunt Becky, a Louisiana Lady, her expression simply an extension of her southern hospitality. Except that her brother might be misbehaving—*he always behaved stupidly if he wasn't constantly being watched*—Jeremy wasn't worried about the *harmless boys* her aunt painted. By now, she realized that the Currie brothers in the police pictures were no one to fear, and that her mother and father, *despite technically breaking the law*, had done their best to protect an innocent pair.

"What did they do?" she dutifully pressed, stalling for time for Keith's return, a ruse unfamiliar to her parents, her blossoming social awareness allowing her into their circle at will.

"Nothin' really, young lady." Her uncle understood her contrivance where the rest were unable, a remarkable insight, since the Klostermans had no children of their own, his intuition making them perfect foils for one-another. And he knew that Keith was on her mind, the twinkle in his eyes—*she recognized this*—a sign that he was on her side. He was convinced that *whatever* Keith was up to, his niece had it covered. "A couple of young outdoorsmen run out of their home, is all. Some think the government cheated them," he paused. "They was cheated, all right. *That's for sure*. But not by no government. It's just that some of them folks live up there out of touch, an—"

"'*Out of touch*', Uncle Neal?" Despite his insight and their mutual understanding, Billie's brown eyes drew him in, her adolescent sparkle laced with an adult charm that he had no hope of escaping.

"Well, they couldn't keep up with coat-and-tie regulations like they should," he winked. "Brothers, ya know. Nice fellas," he brightened. "They lived with their mom up north, he gestured toward their home between Namakan Island and Kettle Falls. "You know the spot, Owen? I know Mary does. Their folks leased it years ago from the Feds like everyone else did; but she was one of the last to give it up. The only one left up there is old Widow Halsey."

Everyone realized that only *some* shoreline and *few* islands within the park were ever private, with *most* real estate on the border now under park service control. Many lots were purchased or acquired through condemnation, while leaseholders were offered a one-time lifetime contract or a settlement for cash. Either way, most buildings were destroyed once abandoned by their owners. Some might be spared due to historic or strategic value; and because of Ted's importance as a coast watcher, he was welcomed to remain in the home he and Jenny had built. But others like the brothers had to leave. Big Timber and some random stretches along southern Sullivan Bay were privately owned, but they were scattered and few.

"Nice fellas," Neal reminisced, "*backward*, I suppose; but we got along fine. They never caused trouble and helped out where they could, *whatever* they could do, which wasn't much. They're fine boys—*mom didn't raise no renegades*—but ain't suited for nothin' that ain't backwoods."

"Their mother taught art in the cities when the boys were babies, *before* Eddie got so sick; and she had someone to watch them." Mary held from declaring Mother Currie's devotion to a son whose illness made him slow. Special schools were considered, but she quit her job instead.

"She painted landscapes. People would come 'round from all

over, an'...*them boys ain't there no more,"* a twist of anger. "'Least not s'posed to be. When she died last year, her sons got run off. Then the forest service leveled their cabin for *more* tourists an' camping an' people who got money," he soured anew, berating the tourism keeping themselves in business.

"I suppose their leases ran out," Owen concluded.

"*Mom's* did, for sure. And they got lost in the shuffle. They was fishermen an' river guides. But guidin' ain't what it was. Now, it's *licensing* an' *bonding*, an' when mom passed on, their back yard turned into *more* of that...*park.*"

"But they were compensated—"

"'*Compensated*'? Hell, no. *Mom* was the one with the lease; although she *did* have plenty of insurance. But where to go? A spot in the cities? With a flower garden out front? An' a picket fence?" he motioned a circle around his coffee cup, his cynicism bitter and open.

"Don't they have friends?"

"*Sure*, they got friends," Neal flared. "But for *what*? To take 'em in? Ol' Gus tried, but they belong on the big water. *Out there,*" he pointed with dramatic irony. *"Especially Eddie* who knows *nothin'* 'bout people."

"What *did* they do, Neal?" Mary realized the two needed to stay together, that Eddie depended on his brother.

"The last we know is some swindler out of Chicago took their mom's insurance money for that bait shop on Big Timber, a slickster named Greenwall."

"Oh, no. Not *Percy* Greenwall!"

"That's the guy," Becky nodded.

"It looked honest, I s'pose. They got a shop in their names—"

"That big overgrown...why, I haven't laid eyes on him—he's *never* here when *we* come up."

"He pokes his nose in here once-in-a-while," Becky admitted.

"The place is run down, and no one goes there anymore—"

"I wish he wouldn't...been back-and-forth for maybe five or six years, now," she sat down next to her sister-in-law.

"Nothin' but a shack."

"In school he was *always* in trouble," Mary recalled.

"No running water or electricity."

"You say he's here?"

"He's around," Neal caught up. "'Cept no one'll deal with him 'cause they're 'fraid of gettin' 'skinned'. Folks figure if ya cross the guy, ya might need to learn to swim."

"Percy was an older classmate," Mary reminisced. "He wasn't popular. He couldn't *do* anything. And in grade school he was mistreated by all the bullies. *It was sad.* No one wanted him on their team. *I remember that.* He would just stand there...*alone*...forced to take whatever they dished out and no one to back him up. I felt sorry for him. The *meaner* boys would spit in his face, and he built up an awful lot of resentment, except...*it never broke his determination.* His father was our banker *until he gave up his job...*," she trailed off, allowing Neal to fill in.

"It was a big misunderstanding. Percy's father was honest. I mean, *he was a damn good banker.* There's folks 'round here who wouldn't have *nothin'* without what he done for 'em. The family don't come back no more, but people support 'em—*the ol' man,* anyway."

"They moved to Chicago, Neal?"

"*Outside* the city. Indiana, actually. Near Chesterton. An' Percy took it hard. *The family* didn't take it hard; but people say Percy soured over the move...that he got bitter an' never had reason, 'cause his dad did well. An' his mom was a good sort, too."

"I wish he'd stay away," Becky repeated.

"We s'pect Percy cheated the boys."

"Maybe worse," she darkened. "And maybe others."

"Yeah...been back and forth...been all over the place, an' *now* he's diggin' in at Walkers."

"What's *'Walkers'*?" Jeremy turned to her aunt, her feigned naiveté. "You mean where Uncle Ted's boat is stored?" She'd been to Ash River often enough to know what *Walkers* meant. By now she and Keith had taken a capricious liking to Gus, and he to them, *as if he was the mysterious grandfather they never knew, a* mutually cautious attraction grown stronger over the years. She knew Freddie stayed there and that Walkers was the oldest dock in the area. But she played the *innocent*, anyway.

"Yes, dear. It's where your uncle's boat stays in the winter."

"Oh," she brightened.

"An' he's got inside help this time. But you explain the rest, Mary. You tell 'bout *Jenny*," Neal faltered as if lost for direction.

Although eager to discuss Percy's interest in Walkers and the *help* that Gus now had, they understood Neal's deeper need...to hear *others* remember his sister, and to recall the details surrounding her death, these reminiscences likened to a Sunday church service. But unlike Ted, Neal's recollections had a vindictive taint, un-tempered by denial: he was convinced that her drowning had been *no accident* and was at the heart of a deeper treachery involving Percy Greenwall.

Mary repeated her part, that Percy's bid for Jenny came before Ted's eyes opened. Ted was slow that way. She laughed at this because Neal's sister outclassed them both. Ted was terrible with the girls, his interests in hunting and fishing outpacing his appreciation for the opposite sex, *until Jenny Klosterman came along*. She smiled, for *Jenny changed Ted's attitude in a hurry*.

But before capturing his attention, there was the Jenny-Percy controversy that neither Mary nor Neal disapproved of, a curiously flat liaison that was neither amorous nor trusting, *the odd couple*, people said, for even *then* the two disagreed. But Percy quarreled with everyone, leaving Jenny discouraged over his lack of control. Mary remembered him as awkward and incompetent and terribly frustrated because he was always dragged into some classroom squabble, manipulated by Zeke Meierson's bullies whose singular aim was to drive *the pinheaded redhead* to the principal's office.

Gawky and gullible, even Percy's sister derogated him, so few could see what Jenny saw: his crude charm and his overwhelming passion for acceptance. Even so, Jennie could see dangerous changes taking place, a new violence strangling his sentient soul. She often spoke with friends about his being twisted into a manipulator of people; but she never thought that one day those frustrations would make even *her* his target.

The Percy-Jenny relationship never had much substance, and in the wake of his father's banking fiasco and their move to Chicago, it dissolved completely. After Percy's departure, the two exchanged mail, with Percy writing notes of expectation and letters of hope because Jenny was closer to him than anyone else had been. In his mind, they remained soul mates. But Jenny's replies were hardly ardent, merely mixtures of explanation and gentle rejection written out of compassion for her troubled classmate. She wrote because Percy had been a friend who deserved *some* consideration.

But that was all.

The rest of the *feelings* had vanished. At least for Jenny Klosterman, they had. What little magic that existed was but a memory, *if there had been any magic at all.*

In the meantime, Jenny and Ted met at his sister's wedding in Berry Falls, a new and compelling experience for Ted because, for the first time in his life, he could speak candidly with a woman outside his own family. Clumsy at first, like navigating the bank of a beaver bog, he soon learned to understand her feminine practicality, her complexity of spirit; and it was *then* when Jenny helped him deal with the passing of his newlywed sister and brother-in-law, and when they grew close and became engaged.

As for Percy, news of Jenny's commitment to Ted was withheld, her letters merely inamorous, dispassionate communications; she felt her marriage plans were none of his business. So when Percy returned to Minnesota to *fan the flame* and to expand his real-estate prospects, the *Jenny and Ted* revelation was an apparent shock to him. *A complete surprise.* Within his aberrations, Percy told anyone with a sympathetic ear that Jenny was *forced* to desert him, that they planned to resume their old affair, and that she had been waiting for *him* the past ten years years, *until another Snelling ruined things.*

Jenny criticized Percy for his claims, and she openly denied them when brought up by others. After all...*ten years!* But deluded by his own fatuity, Percy proclaimed himself cheated, *just as his father had been cheated,* blaming Ted for their split. *Of course,* Ted was to blame. *He was guilty as charged,* and was applauded for his efforts. But in Percy's mind, Ted's *meddling* was more sinister than simple competition: Ted was an upstart who Percy had likened to a thief. *Another hated Snelling. And all of Ted's friends and relatives and all his sawmill pals and ranger buddies emerged as enemies, as well.*

Alarmed by Percy's reaction, Ted advised Jenny to avoid him. But imprisoned amidst memories of their old friendship and her belief that some good remained in the beleaguered banker's boy, Jenny sometimes spoke with him after his return. Theirs were strained and muted conversations, remnants of the days when Percy trusted her and she believed in him. But even *that* was destroyed when she married Ted. Percy was one of the few friends and family members invited to the ceremony; but he held apart, sullen and disconsolate, watching and plotting from afar, *revenge* his secret mission. On the surface he continued to confide in her; but his *front* fell into a false and dangerous confidence that nearly everyone misunderstood.

Later, when Jenny confronted him for some questionable business dealings, he clouded, warning her to stay out of his affairs; when she criticized him for cheating her friends, he turned angry and warned her some more; and when she finally threatened to report him for a particularly dishonest maneuver, he at last had his fill. *Her meddling had to stop.*

Without witnesses, that day's events remained capsulated by unofficial guesswork: One afternoon while Ted was away on business, Percy made a surreptitious run up the river. Hours later, fishermen discovered Jenny's empty boat within the narrows. Despite a week-long search, she was never found; and without contrary evidence, her death was ruled an accident. But Neal was unconvinced. She'd told him in confidence that she'd overheard an argument between Percy and a swindled client, and that it worried her. Neal regretted not watching her more carefully when Ted was away. And it didn't matter that Percy was seen fishing far from the cabin that evening, because of all the angling Percy had done, he was no fisherman.

"An' nobody who *really* knows that crook will talk to him, 'cept Gus an' his daughter, an' that young fella workin' for him," Neal concluded.

Gus Walkinen, the postmaster and the oldest dock owner on Ash River, had more land and money than he needed, *with a heart of gold to match.* His helper was a malfeasor named Freddie Moore, a troubled city youth and an alley runner when pushed. During his stay with Gus, Freddie grew attached to Percy, doting on his cheap-jack adult-hero with a mix of acceptance and suspicion common among his street friends, extracting from Percy what he could use and discarding the rest.

Inspired by Percy, Freddie began sneaking out at night, *too late for Gus to monitor,* seeking out shady friends like the rich Meierson boys on Black Duck Road while the elder Meiersons spent their days building boats in Duluth *and their nights on the town.* Everyone knew the Meiersons supplied their boys with a guardian (who only infrequently reviewed the boys' behavior) and a groundskeeper and every material contrivance they wanted, but had little time for their sons who ran the roost and caused trouble on the docks, while *they* made money and did their thing in the city.

Freddie understood all this: his parents didn't have the cash the Meiersons squandered. But they *did* have the time, and they squandered *that* with little trouble.

Percy observed this arrangement while comparing the Meierson complication, *even Freddie's unique situation,* to his own. Of course, *that* was a stretch, Percy's misconduct having little to do with being neglected. But the rationalization presented an opportunity to befriend Freddie on terms too tempting to ignore. Condemning the Meiersons was the *proper* thing to do. Whether Gus bought the act or not, was debatable, for Gus was an excellent judge of character. Unfortunately, while Percy held Roxanne in tow, Gus applauded him, implicitly condoning Percy's influence on Freddie Moore.

Freddie remained pleasant around his benefactor. He liked Gus. In contrast, he followed Percy only warily. Freddie was intelligent, reasonably dependable, and an asset to the dock owner for his skill with marine engines. It was at Walkers where Ted's spare and motor were stored, the craft the Petersons would take to Ted's, and one of the boats Freddie maintained.

Neal continued, "Course, Percy an' Freddie hit it off, 'cause Gus looks the other way," he grimaced. "An' *that was him,*" he turned to Jeremy. "That was Freddie you an' Keith was runnin' with a while ago. What d'ya think of him?"

Jeremy shrugged, "He left in such a hurry when I told him who we were." Despite her act, *Jeremy was worried.* She was worried that her brother had gotten lost or had fallen in the river. A million things had run through her mind since leaving him at Donavan Marsh until—*just then*—they all saw him bouncing up and down in front of the bay window, *acting like an idiot again.* "I thought he acted kinda strange—"

"He just 'left' ya?"

"*Who?* Oh, *Yes.* He said he 'had to go'," her brown eyes darted.

"Did he say where to?"

"No. I told him who we were and where we're going this evening, and all of a sudden *he had to go.* Then I saw him start up a boat a while later and head down the river," she pointed.

"That's odd. He's s'posed to help Gus get *your* boat ready. I said to him to tell Gus that you folks was here," the furrows on Neal's forehead deepened. "Why, hell, an' that ol' barge has been floatin' in the shed for only a week…been dry docked all winter," he fretted. They knew Gus would struggle with setting up and sealing the wooden craft himself, he and Owen sharing a knowing glance.

"What does Ted think?" Mary asked.

"'Ted'? 'Bout *what?* '*Bout the boat?*"

"No, *of course not*," she looked irritated

"Oh…'bout the kid, you mean."

"No. *About Percy, for goodness sakes.*" Hardly focused on some local youth, Mary remembered Percy being outmaneuvered by her brother and complaining about the money the Snellings had. And she would politely listen, despite being a Snelling herself.

"Aw, I know what you mean. Ted tolerates that ol' crook, like he puts up with *everyone else* around here. I don't understand him sometimes. But it ain't just Percy I worry about. It's Gus's daughter who's a cat-in-a-bag with all those fellas she smuggles in. *She's* the one ya watch out for."

"*His daughter?*"

"*Sure*, his daughter. Lately she's stayin' with her Aunt Ida on Iron Bay—*been there for years*—but still spends plenty of time at her dad's."

"You mean, *Roxanne?* His *step-daughter*, you mean. That spoiled brat. Her own mother ran her out." Mary disliked Roxanne and wondered why Ida and Gus catered to her, all the while recalling that Roxanne was *her own age and a close friend at one time.*

At one time, Roxanne had it all…pretty, well-to-do, and a crowd-pleaser. In school she was popular, afraid of nothing, *especially on a dare.* But she sported the lowest grades in her small class despite cheating with regularity. Unconcerned about her future, she would flaunt her long hair and brag about her father being *the richest man on the river.* When they were young, Roxy and Jenny were best friends, sharing their fears and dreams like young girls do. Even their families got along. The Snellings, too, although *that* molded like bad cheese when Roxy's mother revealed to her that *her father was Mary Snelling's very own Uncle Cyrus.* This was a difficult pill; but it was made even worse when her mother admitted telling Cyrus to get out of her life.

Mary remembered Roxanne being *devastated* by that news. She wasn't upset about frayed relations, and she cared nothing about old man Cyrus. Rather, Roxy realized that despite having Snelling blood within her, there would *never* be any Snelling money; and it struck her like a bolt that there'd be no share in her mother's *Richardson* wealth, either—*at least, not yet.* But the *coup de grace* came when she found out that Gus, *who was not even her step-father,* never adopted her, this unforgivable exclusion forcing her attitude to plummet like a stump over Kettle Falls because all her bragging in school had been wasted. With her mother's bad news, she'd become a fallen star, an outcast angel, the dramatization totally inaccurate except in her own mind. Embittered over the perception that she'd been deceived by her parents, she turned on *everyone* including *her own best friends.*

Roxy was never the little princess imagined in her looking glass land; rather, with her *fall,* she became a wild thing, a party girl, contemptuous of the law, although slowed down with her friends around. She was careful to hide *that* side of herself, but not so careful that Jenny couldn't see. Jenny disapproved of her *slide* but said little because Roxanne was still her friend. Even after her mother's loss was revealed (Cyrus never knew Roxanne beyond infancy, and had no knowledge of her turmoil), her hatred for the Snellings was suppressed. But Jenny and her friends caught on: their first falling out was in high school when she—*Mary*—was blamed for stealing another girl's billfold. Soon discovered, Jenny reproached Roxy who apologized for the theft. But like a bully without buddies, her dark side unveiled, her bad habits led to a breakup with Jenny and Mary and the rest of her friends.

Roxanne's spiral continued after graduation, with Mary and Jenny attending the University at Duluth, then returning each summer to assist with their families' businesses. *But not Roxanne.* For her, there was no college and no help for a would-be stepfather unable to claim her. Instead, she attached herself to a string of goldbrickers until she and her current runabout were encouraged to remove themselves to one of Ida's cabins on Iron Bay. By then, Mary and Owen were married and settled in the cities. But Mary remembered hearing of Ida's impenetrable patience with Roxanne and her shady companions, and of their squabbling over money. Nevertheless, the two ladies got along, *with Gus paying the bills,* and Ida turning blind to her niece's improprieties.

Meanwhile, Ted's friendship with Jenny culminated in their marriage at the grotto near Cross Corner, with only a few friends and family members attending. But it came to a bitter end a year later when Jenny's boat was found among the rocks of the narrows near her home.

"That's right," Neal grumped. "Gus don't have family. She's his only heir. She ain't much, but she's all he's got."

"That's a problem?"

"*Not for her*, it ain't. She'll get it all, anyway—*unless Percy steals it*. Or unless Gus wakes up to who *should* get it," he glanced involuntarily at Jeremy.

"And *that's the problem*," Becky repeated, "because Gus is *just like Ted.* He thinks *everyone* has a good side if you look hard enough for it."

"Ya gotta look damn hard in her case," Neal grumbled.

"Well…she *is* his daughter—"

"His little gold-digger, ya mean. *She ain't even his real daughter.* An' where's *Percy's* good side? He ain't got one—"

"Oh, Neal, that's not like you," Mary chided.

"Well, have ya ever seen his good side? So, wouldn't you know it? Ol' Gus turns to *Percy* to patch things up. Damdest lookin' couple. *Percy and Roxanne.* If he'd keep his nose out of their business, maybe they'd drown each other. Ya know, give 'em some rope—"

"*Who* should keep his nose out?" Mary assumed he meant Gus.

"Well…*Ted.*"

"*Ted?*" she bristled at the thought of her brother consorting with Roxanne. "*What do you mean, 'Ted'?*"

"By givin' advice where it ain't appreciated."

"Oh, I don't believe—"

"Oh, *sure* you do. An', *yes he has.* An' warnin' Gus 'bout Percy."

Mary frowned but realized that this was very much like her Good Samaritan brother, *appreciated or not.* "But why would anyone—"

"Have *her?*" Neal snorted. "For Gus's money...and his land along the river," he waved. "Percy's pullin' strings with *lots* of people—with them Currie boys, for damn sure. Remember the Cormorant Falls *Johansons,* an' how when they moved here, Molly don't know walleye from sauger, an' how they bought land on lower Sullivan without checkin' it out? 'Cept Percy never had access to Sullivan land. *Hah!* Least, *not yet,* he don't—*an' how they lost their down payment?* Then, 'bout Big Bear Resort near where Rainy River empties? Where Riley Abrams got caught in the Pottsbourg quicksand—"

"And had to sit there—" Mary started.

"—*up to his neck* 'till his wife went lookin'," Neal brightened. "An' how the owner of the place don't have title 'cause Percy faked the deed! Then how he run out when the law caught on?"

"What?" Owen mouthed.

"That's right. *Just ask around.*" Then he pressed, "But ya gotta flag Ted down this time 'cause when Roxanne turns forty real soon, people say Gus has her lined up for half-ownership, although...*nothin' on paper.* But that's a lot of *ownership* to lose, even if it *ain't* on paper. If Percy's bested *again* by your brother, no tellin' *what'll* happen."

Mary agreed, then turned, "What does Ted think about the Curries?" She worried over the connection between Percy and the brothers, perhaps their fate *already* sealed.

"Oh, he don't know. He *talks* like they're around, if anyone'll listen. Sometimes we repeat stories, *or hear what we want to hear.* But none of us seen 'em for some time. Not the whole past year, we haven't."

Becky nodded.

"It's like they dropped off the edge," he motioned. "An' I don't care *nothin'* 'bout *tipsters* an' *local taverns,*" he sneered, "or in the cities, for God's sake. Was it last year fishermen spied smoke an' a tarpaper lean-to on their island? The Forest Service tore down their cabin, ya know. They leveled the place clean, an' burned it all in the bargain."

"So, what happened?"

"'So what happened' was a couple rangers went up to investigate—just after you folks left—*an' they get shot at!* Can you figure the Currie boys shootin' at their friends? *What are people thinking?*" He thumped the table in denial.

Owen offered, "But no one *witnessed* the shooting?"

"Nope. Can't say they did. It's like...*who did it? Who was really there?* An' that attorney last fall? How they found his boat is all?"

A young Federal man sent in to monitor the area had gone missing. Others were assigned to the legalities of land transitions, but *this* agent, people said, was watching Percy who was at the heart of several unique problems; but after a week of work, he disappeared. The group at Klostermans reminded each other that each evening the attorney checked messages at his motel, but after failing to show for two days, officials were notified. A week later, a cut-and-paste ransom demand mailed from Gus's post office appeared at the station, and a payoff of marked bills was made. But nothing was spent, and neither he nor the kidnappers were heard from again.

"I hear they found some of that cash *on Currie property,*" Owen's reference to Big Timber.

Yeah, well, don't forget where that lawyer's boat wound up."

"On Currie Island?" Hardly a guess, it was a well-advertised bit of evidence.

"Yup. Tied to the rocks at their old place, an' just lookin' for attention."

Chapter 5

When Gus Walkinen and Zita Richardson announced their marriage plans forty years ago, the news was followed by a deluge of criticism and doubt. *Friends* of the families, older folks who never knew them well, fretted over the Walkinen wealth, fearing that Gus's inheritance would fall into unscrupulous hands—*not their hands*, of course—while others pointed to Roxanne, Zita's precocious two-year-old, deciding that Zita was getting restless again and needed a break and wouldn't mind pocketing some Walkinen dollars on her way out.

Few sympathized, and even fewer knew Gus's mind, most agreeing that the young landowner was lonely and was being used by Zita. Most concluded that once finished with him, she would dispose of him; while others grumped that he should know better than to consort with *that* sort of trouble. Sure, Gus was lonely: they understood his predicament. And, of course, he needed companionship. But they all warned him that Zita was the wrong choice.

But the conventional skeptics with their conservative wisdom would be proven wrong, for the *older* and *wiser* soon found Gus's determination to win Zita's heart and the devotion he and Zita shared outstripping their *wisdom* or power to condemn.

Years earlier, Gus's parents, Finnish immigrants, purchased a tract of Ash River shoreline from the government when logging was young and land was cheap, then improved part of their property as a landing and trading station. Their spot, dubbed *Walkers*, was renamed *Walkers Landing* by the postal service as people began settling nearby. Soon, local businesses served an influx of forest workers; and when hotel owners and *resorteers* joined in, land values soared and fortunes were made. But for many, it was a difficult, undisciplined existence, the winters often intolerable. By the time Gus turned thirty, his parents had worked themselves into a small fortune and early graves, leaving him land and property and an emptiness he longed to fill.

Summers were profitable for the young man, a hard worker and as equally industrious as were his parents; but in the off-seasons, life turned cold and lonely, the monotony broken only by infrequent encounters with year-'rounders and natives, or with trappers and traders passing through.

Few were permanent on the river. One family with roots as deep as the Walkinens' were the Richardsons. Eb Richardson, along with Ted and Mary Snelling's grandfather, were fire-tower forest rangers, so they were fixtures of sorts, as well as Neal

Klosterman's grandparents who operated a trading station nearby.

As a young ranger, Ted's father canoed up Ash River each morning to an inlet called Skunk Creek. From there, as Ted told the story, his father traveled upstream on Skunk for three-quarter mile to a hilltop clearing surrounding an eighty foot fire tower. In mountainous country the lofty, hundred-foot observation rooms were sometimes accessible by enclosed stairways, but not so with the Skunk Creek tower with its caged ladder on the outside, a precarious access, and not intended for the faint-hearted.

Climbing to his lonely lookout with the day's supplies strapped to his back, Virgil Snelling's job was to watch for smoke and to triangulate on hot spots with an *alidade*, a sighting instrument mounted on a circular table lying within a map of the area and equipped with a degree ring used to plot direction. With his own tower spotted exactly at the center of his map, he would report compass bearings, distances, and the size of each fire to the central station by land line or radio. If other rangers reported the same trouble spot, a fix could be plotted on the main map at headquarters, and a firefighting team could then be sent out. Using their radios, towermen could also communicate with each other; and they got to know each other. This was important for the workers, for despite being a busy and dangerous job when lightning storms were brewing, or during the camping season when the weather was dry, it could also be a tedious stay.

From the start, Gus was betaken by Eb's attractive but misbehaved daughter, Zita. At first, he struggled to turn her precocious eye, having lived his life as a bachelor and knowing only the social graces coming from common sense. But Gus was likeable. Courteous and good-looking, he soon won her over with his humor and charm—*although not to everyone's delight.* It was her curiosity with his hard work and attention to detail that *initially* attracted her; and as he persisted, she recognized a moral individualism in this young man that was one-of-a-kind and worth pursuing.

However, not everyone was convinced. It was "…only because she's in trouble again," old Royland Klosterman complained to anyone within earshot in his effort to keep young Gus from making "…a big mistake."

At least that's what Royland said.

But it was more complicated than Roy let on, for the elder Klosterman knew that Zita had been seeing Ted's influential Uncle Cyrus on more than a *friendly* basis. Cyrus was a local politician and, unknown to many, *he fathered her child.* For personal reasons and for business and financial concerns that he shared with Cyrus, Royland tried warning Gus away.

Instead of *agreeing* with Roy, Eb should have taken offense, like *any* father would: *it was none of Royland's business what Zita did.* But Eb was a hard-bitten old fool whose weakness for money-comforts prevented him from understanding his own daughter…*from understanding more than what Royland would allow.* Eb *refused* to understand because there was no profit in understanding. Instead, coming from the old school where wives were obliged to *hold their tongue* and where children did as *father knows best,* Eb argued that his daughter was headed for the *wrong side;* and he threatened to disown her if she continued to encourage Gus. But long past controlling his twenty-four-year-old, Eb's major concern was that Congressman Snelling might frown on Gus's meddling and scuttle a lumbermill deal that he—*Eb*—and Royland were finalizing with some Berry Falls partners. He was afraid the congressman would follow up his threats to start *his own* firm, and that he'd drop his daughter like a bale of alfalfa if young Gus interfered.

Despite his hard-edged heritage and *old school* traditions, Eb's threats were unnecessarily closed-minded, for he never considered that *Cyrus* might have slipped onto the *wrong side* or that Royland had no business in his daughter's affairs. Never once had he considered that Gus and Zita might *really* be in love, or that Gus might be a better business pal than any of the Snelling or Klosterman crew.

At first, Cyrus, who was twenty years Zita's senior, fooled everyone. He was rich and powerful, so *that* was easy, especially with Eb, for *Eb was a fool.* After flatly denying he'd complicated Zita's life with a child, Cyrus magnanimously announced that he would do "…whatever I can for the little girl," all the while declaring that matrimony was "…not part of my agenda."

Agenda, indeed.

Despite her father's approval of the congressman's tactics and Royland's manipulations, Zita was outraged by Cyrus's infidelity;

she promptly retaliated by proclaiming Cyrus's parentage and declaring *her own* split with him, this doing little for his local reputation, *or her bank account*. Her declaration put Gus at odds with Cyrus and gave validity to old Roy's contention that Zita could be trouble when she wanted to be. It also gave Ebeneezer just cause to write her out of his will.

Gus was never swayed, nor did he feel that *he* was on the *wrong side*. He reasoned that Zita had no need to *kowtow* to Cyrus or to her infected father, *or to Royland Klosterman*, for that matter. He felt she was never a problem, nor the vagrant that Eb portrayed; rather Gus felt she'd been misused by Cyrus, unfairly castigated by Royland, and carelessly chastised by her own father.

To the surprise of Eb and his cronies, *to the surprise of the told-you-so brimstone breathers,* Zita and Gus were soon deeply and faithfully attached to each other. In spite of some lingering criticism, it was obvious their love was as real as Eb's threats were unfair.

But packed with irony and unknowns, life reared back to prove its unpredictability, for it wasn't Zita *or Cyrus* with whom Gus's problems would spring; rather, it was Cyrus's offspring, Roxanne, with whom Gus would meet his ultimate challenge.

Roxanne wasn't told who her father was until she was sixteen. She was a difficult child, anyway; but with *that* disclosure, Cyrus's corruption underscored her heritage: turning mercenary and dishonest, Roxanne became his perfect progeny. To many, *she* inspired Gus and Zita to inaugurate their Summer House for young runaways, their dedication to youth-in-confusion born of an inability to temper their own charge. Ironically, their own charge, *their only child*, was a prototype for the many kids entering their doors over the next two decades.

Years passed. And difficulties mounted. By the time she was twenty-five, Roxanne had been twice married and separated, and was often in trouble. Still at home, she'd run up a string of debts the ailing Zita could no longer tolerate. After a stormy argument one evening, she'd walked out spouting an oath that she'd stay with her Aunt Ida Richardson on Iron Bay. This was acceptable for everyone—*until the day her latest drinking companion turned sober, gave up, and moved out, and Percy Greenwall moved in.*

Percy was no newcomer to the docks: he'd been back-and-forth for several years giving Jenny and her friends a bad time, although his family was better remembered along the river. Most considered his father a gracious and reputable businessman who'd been the victim of local politics…*of Cyrus Snelling politics.*

When Banker Greenwall had approved financing for Roy and Eb's lumbermill some years back, he'd secured it with deeds to timberland planned to support the operation. But opposition had come from a state legislator named Cyrus Snelling, Ted's incorrigible uncle. If Cyrus had kept his position and controversy with Zita out of the fray and remained an honest businessman this time around, he might have survived. But he'd been infected by the dollar virus. Bitter over criticism from Eb's daughter, and upset that Eb failed to keep Gus away, he'd promoted *his own* mill, with no intention of allowing Eb-and-company to interfere. Then using his office to *investigate* Eb's holdings, Cyrus discovered (against Brother Virgil's wishes) that one mortgaged parcel was leased, and another not wholly owned, this *uncovering of improprieties* becoming a media event, the controversy leading to an examination by banking officials and a subsequent demand by *selected* depositors for Greenwall's dismissal, *with Cyrus fanning the flames all along the way.*

Of course, Eb's lumbermill plans had been scuttled, this failed deal resulting in a feud between the Snelling and the Richardson supporters, a kind of *Hatfield and McCoy* fracas that went unresolved until Cyrus was driven from public service with his conviction for bribery in a road building project.

Ted and Nancy (Mary was too young yet to know local politics) hadn't been surprised by any of this, little admiring Uncle Cyrus, anyway. The old legislator and his younger brother were so *unalike*—Virgil, a soft-spoken outdoorsman, and Cyrus, a self-centered stuffed-shirt—that their father once quipped, "at least he keeps to the cities where he belongs."

Mostly, Cyrus *did* stay in the cities; his only tie with Brother Virgil was their partnership in the lumbermill that the Richardson group had planned to compete against. But even in the spirit of *competition,* Virgil found his brother's tactics unfair. He knew the elder Greenwall was an honest banker who'd been dealt an unwarranted blow. Few tears were shed when Cyrus was finally undone.

With the Snelling brothers gone, sawmill memories would have faded except that Gus and friends continued admiring the benevolent banker for his character and family values. So when Percy returned, he was able to wave the flag of fair play, thus inheriting Gus's trust by default...*a good start for the young realtor.* But Percy's was a short-lived victory: he simply wasn't up to the task, vengeance and greed controlling his emotions. Nevertheless, Gus trusted him, although not with the same loyalty allowed his father. In turn, *Gus's* behavior infuriated his friends because Percy and the elder Greenwall were cut from different stone. *Couldn't Gus see that?* Instead, encouraged by Percy and Roxanne's *attraction,* Gus saw the banker's boy as a conciliatory link between himself and his stepdaughter. For *his* part, young Greenwall realized that Gus intended to make her a partner (*who else* might he give his property to?), thus giving Percy an opportunity to *prove* himself in his own deceitful way.

Gus's generosity and Zita's compassion had been legendary, their kindness affecting many families across the state. But for Roxanne, *legend* wasn't filling her pockets. Gus's failure at adoption and her mother's inability to control the Richardson purse strings would always be a cause for deception.

For Percy, *there were no excuses.* Gus soon turned wary of him, but *that* was no sin because everyone harbored the same doubts. However, Gus was never unkind: he'd never crossed the young man, and he'd always respected the Greenwall name. But *none of that* for Percy Greenwall, for *Gus was old and rich and easy,* and Roxy was too convenient a tool to pass up.

In fact, the two understood each other intimately if not *intimately,* neither trusting the other any more than required. So with suspicious hearts and larceny in their souls, the pair put twisted smiles on their faces and set about, arm-in-arm, to claim their grandest prize of all.

Chapter 6

It was late, and the Petersons were pressed to get underway. Without phone service at the cabin, radio communications were all they had; but since they planned to surprise Ted, there was no reason to go on air. So they said good-bye to Neal and Becky and advised them they'd return in a week, then drove to Walkers Landing a half-mile down shore. Passing a new service station, several antique shops, a generic gift emporium that had just sprung up, two new hotels made to look rustic and weathered, a re-faced jewelry store, and a candy depot selling more gold than did the jewelry outlet, Mary marveled at the changes on River Drive, *even since last year,* and wondered what it would look like when Keith and Jeremy were grown, refusing to acknowledge that Jeremy was *already* grown, that her daughter might not come this way again. Up the road, as two bridges crossed branches of Ash River where the water pushed into bays, the Petersons wound through a half-mile-long campground filled with camper-trailers likened to mobile homes. Mary worried that establishments like Walkers Landing and Klostermans Bar and Café might soon be gone and was saddened by the changes the park inspired.

The *landing*, a wooden, two-story structure that looked out of place with nearby additions and renovations, included Gus's residence in the balconied upper, with the post office and his old-fashioned marina comprising the ground floor. In addition to his dockside duties, Gus was the postmaster and a river guide whenever energy and opportunity allowed. At one time his place housed the ranger station, but that was moved for lack of space and accessibility. Alongside his establishment, bleached-gray for want of paint, lay strewn assorted debris, an old foot-powered and out-of-round grinding wheel leaning precariously against the wall of a shed housing garden tools, a rice-parching drum, and dated irrigation equipment; while the vegetable garden Zita once cared for, now a fenced-in, weed-infested plot behind the buildings, remained unused since her death.

"Can't figure it," Gus puzzled through his tobacco-beard. "He was just here...poked his nose in the door a half hour ago like he always does. That young pup knew he had work to do," Gus grumped, trying to look stern; but it was only the kindness in his hazel-deep eyes that shone through, a gray, faraway gaze setting off his wizened, lonesome ways, a fractured, once broken-hearted look he chose neither to repair nor to apologize for.

The Petersons were running late, so Owen helped Gus maneuver Ted's spare from its enclosed mooring, a piling-supported garage-on-water wherein hung the malignant odor of gasoline and decayed wood and dead fish, all the while Gus muttering to himself, "...where that young fella run off to again." Freddie was a newcomer, with Gus more worried about his safety than the work he neglected. He was worried that Freddie had gotten lost or had fallen overboard while showing off for one of his young lady friends downriver. Privately, Gus considered those *lady friends* more capable of *showing off* than Freddie was, for all of which Gus preferred to keep him away from *that* kind of trouble: Freddie had plenty-enough problems as it was. Despite his urban background and the bluster he splashed around, Gus considered Freddie more backward than most of the local youth who'd never approached a high rise or been awed by city lights.

For years, Gus and his wife ran a county funded haven for kids, an earn-your-own-way bed-and-bath where he and Zita encouraged positive behavior. With nowhere to turn, many youths found themselves with a job on the docks and a home in the rambling upper at Walkers Landing. Even after his wife passed away and Gus could no longer fulfill county requirements, his offer for employment attracted someone like Freddie Moore.

"Didn't figure settin' up the old barge today, anymore," Gus peered at his pocket watch, his pause more out of habit than a check of the time, for the railroad timepiece ran notoriously slow. It was given to him by a retired Duluth-to-Winnipeg engineer whom he'd befriended while on a fishing excursion—*K.C. Jones,* by coincidence. K.C. was a fiery-haired, barrel-chested Irishman who, with his wife and son, took a liking to Gus at first sight. "At my age," Gus repeated the familiar, "who worries about time, anyhow," he guffawed, a curious concoction of laughter, cough, and throat scrubbing that sounded like a flushing toilet. Then he added, "Ted said you folks would show tomorrow." He now rehearsed his poorly executed gruff-and-gravel show, thereby rejecting any Peterson reply, while stuffing his watch into the coin pocket of his tattered coveralls and lapsing again into wondering, "...where that young fella's hiding out." Drawing from Gus's puzzlement, Owen determined that not only were Freddie and a rental boat missing, but several life jackets, as well, although neither he nor Owen drew the irregularities together, nor could they know of the drama unfolding under their noses.

Ted's spare, a heavy, wooden, sixteen-footer was a *one-of-a-kind* on the river. Old and reliable—*and large enough for their needs*—there were once many similar to it, but no longer; and when Mary recognized it as one she rode in it as a child, he nodded, "Could be, you bet. This big ol' barge's been 'round a long while, 'an 'bout the only one like it up here anymore. Now-days they're made of aluminum or some other fancy stuff," his voice cracked to match his weathered face. Prior to this trip, the Petersons had always used one of the *fancy stuff* varieties, aluminum or fiberglass, that Gus had on hand; and on one excursion, they set out in one of Neal's rental crafts too small for their needs. "I believe your granddad owned it. He took care of it, too," he proudly added. "But you'd had trouble this time," he revealed, "what with that load you got," he gave a critical glance at the uncommon mound of luggage atop their car parked in the lot across the road. If the boat had been any smaller, Owen realized that some of their belongings would need to be left behind, perhaps for another trip or abandoned completely. *It wouldn't be the first time,* he recalled the berry buckets hauled north each year, sometimes getting stored in Gus's boat shack or under the back steps of the cabin if they survived the trip at all, *and he privately criticized Mary for wanting to bring more of them along.* Ideally, they'd have taken *two* boats but they had no one to run with them, and Owen ruled Mary out. "Don't know what made such a thing, but there's a fresh hole back there," he scratched his stubbled chin. "It would 'a swamped you folks if ya stopped for anything out there," he pointed to a spot below the stern planking. "But we'll seal it up proper…plug it up good…won't cause no trouble fer ya," he promised, shuffling along in a pair of laceless boots that looked like a pair of misused bedroom slippers.

While Gus and Owen made repairs to the boat and tested the old Evinrude, Mary and the kids purchased lantern fuel and perishables from the general store next door, as well as snacks and soft drinks and toiletries, some of which Ted would have found little use for. They then laboriously transferred their luggage and supplies—*and Owen's brand-new gas-powered trolling motor*—from the car to the craft, all the while heeding Gus's caution to "…tie loose things down in case the wind comes up," and to "…stow heavy gear up front. 'An stay out of the bow seat when the water's rough," he reminded them, smiling at the kids with a Dusty-like grin, "'cause the waves'll shake yer teeth loose." He was worried not only about Freddie's disappearance, but that the weather was taking a turn. The wind had picked up from out of the north and it was getting colder, an ominous sign on the big water, and a poor time for a green crew with a laden-down boat to be heading into the late-afternoon boundary waters wilderness.

Finally, after donning life jackets hanging within a *vest rack* out front (Gus found the preservers to be in unusually short supply), and with Dusty perched between Keith and Jeremy at the center seat and attached to Jeremy by a short leash, the Petersons bid good-by to Gus and departed for Ted's cabin ten miles upriver.

Churning their way out of the resort area, looking like a loaded cargo barge on the Mississippi, the Petersons found the river broadening into *Gray Lake*, a first link in one of the many chains spanning the state's northern tier, a glacier-carved string of basins draining northward into Hudson Bay. This widened stretch of Ash River wasn't *Gray Lake* on any map, rather it was a local name reflecting cliffs of exposed bedrock rising randomly like garrison guards along the way. The entire area lay within the southern extension of the Canadian Shield, with some of the oldest formations in the world, making the *guards* as ancient as the last four glaciers that had carved them. Since the last *ice*, a delicate layer of soil had accumulated to support the undergrowth of red and white pine and the slender jack pine used for pulpwood, as well as the Canadian balsam and Douglas fir that the Petersons gazed upon as they forged along. Within the length of shallow Gray Lake pushed the Ash River channel running its hidden course to the lake's constriction at its far end. Sticking to this proven waterway to avoid bridge pilings in the dock area where a forestry road once crossed, or over shallow sand bars as the river widened, Owen navigated the heavy craft along the familiar route leading to Uncle Ted's narrows on Kabetogema Lake where hundreds of rocky islands and a myriad of coves and bays were scattered.

Among the trees blanketing the shoreline, cabins were visible on bedrock outcrops or nestled within protected bays, the topography rugged and varied with rolling hills interspersed among bogs, beaver ponds, swamps, and islands large and small. Hidden by their rustic construction of log and rock, each cabin was complimented by its floating dock serving as driveway and port-of-call for visitors. South of the park boundary and on the lower extremities of Gray Lake, some of the homes were privately-owned, year-round structures, while others provided summer retreat for those whose occupations called them away each winter, or for those whom that bitter clime presented no attraction.

Presently, shouting over the outboard's drone, and pointing through the cold spray of the open water, Owen motioned toward the apparent *bay* they were about to enter, and that part of the trip Keith remembered best. First appearing as another wooded inlet, the *bay* abruptly opened narrow, deep, and dangerous to reveal the ancient handiwork of their hidden river, a timeless, gorge-like gap cutting through cliffs of gray bedrock rising imposingly on both sides of a bottleneck waterway, the near-mile-long pass through which boats were compelled to navigate as they slipped from the confines of Gray Lake—*Sullivan Bay on the map*—to the open waters beyond.

Reducing his speed in a quartering bout with the wind, then slowing to a crawl as they entered the passage, Owen took heed of the flat, submerged shelves extending several feet from each rock wall. More than one boat, *usually traveling too fast,* met its fate here and he had no desire to join the rest. The *latest* had occurred two weeks earlier when, near sundown, a dated pontoon craft owned by a local guide service had punctured one of its rusted floats, and its party of nine had to be rescued by passers-by.

"Careful, Owen," Mary worried as the kids hung on.

"I know, Mary. Keep an eye out for those ledges," he pointed, feeling like one of the two-century-old canoe adventurers who might have traveled south into these waters, the French-Canadian *Voyageurs,* for whom the park was named.

On a calm day, the ledges could be seen below, but through the waves, his gaze riveted only on where the shelves *should* have been. They had a wide berth, and he knew that with their engine idled down, a collision would cause little damage. Of course, extra caution couldn't hurt; but a quarter of the way through the gorge, there came trouble of *another* variety, for soon after throttling down, their big engine sputtered, ran roughly for a few moments, then like an ill-tuned car on the freeway, *it died.* When Owen tried re-starting the old outboard, it apparently required more attention than he could give. Looking around for assistance, *a mechanic,* he realized that but for a solitary fisherman anchored a half-mile south, they were alone on the lake, *stranded.* It never occurred to him to wonder what a fisherman was doing in the shallows of Sullivan Bay. He knew fishing was poor in *that* location, and once out of the channel, getting hung up on a sand bar was a real possibility.

"*Stalled?*" Mary echoed. "*How can that be?* I thought Gus had that motor worked on. *What do we do now?*" she worried as her brother's familiar warnings came to mind.

"*Let's get the spare on!*" Owen ordered as they maneuvered supplies and equipment to make room. "This thing better work," he added under his breath, wondering what was next if the little engine failed to perform.

While they struggled, a story repeatedly told by one of Gus's friends raced through Owen's mind, an uncomfortably humorous anecdote about two woodsmen friends hauling supplies from a nearby landing to a remote site where a cabin was being built. They were using two boats but had only one life jacket to share between them. In the days when life preservers were poorly constructed and unreliable, and when boating regulations were rarely enforced, both men were all-the-more apprehensive of the open water because neither could swim. To solve their dilemma, they contrived to depart with their loads in relays; then while passing each other, they would throw the jacket from one boat to the other, so that—*for whatever it was worth*—on the open water, each might possess that sacred piece of survival gear. But on one particular pass, the jacket slipped and fell into the water and…*it sank like a brick,* the story went, among tears of laughter and bottles of beer around the old oak table at Walkers Landing.

As Owen thought about that likely-embellished incident, he mounted the spare, a gasoline-powered fishing motor he received for Christmas the year before, only a two-horse and never used until today. He had no occasion to use it until now, *especially at the ballpark*, he wryly considered. But as the Petersons were being blown about within the gorge, the little engine sputtered to life with enough power to slowly, safely move them along again.

And so their trip went.

Then, *at last*, off to the east as they emerged from the mile-long pass, there appeared in the distance Uncle Ted's Rocky Point. Not as imposing as other similarly named Rocky Points, it nevertheless stood out as a conspicuous part of Ted's front yard, a readily-visible landmark for travelers along Kabetogema's south shore.

At the north end of the point, near where it narrowed to a wedge-like peak, was constructed a metal tower topped with a high-intensity, battery-and-solar strobe that Ted checked each evening. A path ran from Ted's front porch to a security fence surrounding the park service beacon, then continued higher to a shortwave radio antenna at the point's apex.

Ted's log cabin was set among the trees, hidden from view from the mouth of Ash River a half mile west. When it finally appeared this evening, framed by red-orange remnants of a setting sun, it did so from out of nowhere, looming high, golden, and ruggedly majestic, *the crown of Rocky Point*.

"Finally!" Mary announced as her brother's bay appeared. Because of their load and the small engine they were forced to rely

on, it took twenty minutes to get from the river's outlet to her brother's dock, a seemingly endless trip as they plowed along on the choppy lake.

But despite Mary's relief, the Petersons soon found things amiss, for as they crawled from the broken waters of Kabetogema into Ted's protected dock area, Ted and his dog were not there to greet them. Usually Puck would lead the way with his ears flapping as he rollicked down the rampway to *investigate* or to ward off the uninvited—*and Puck knew the difference*. He was an especially valuable guard at night when the intruder might be a black bear searching for food or a porcupine looking to get inside. Once when Ted and Nancy had gone to the falls for the night, a bear had broken the back door latch and destroyed a store of honey in the pantry, a mess taking days to repair.

"Where's Puck?" Keith wondered, his eyes searching up and down the suspended rampway.

"Where's Uncle Ted?" Jeremy followed.

"I don't know," her mother answered. Then she turned to Owen, "You suppose he's out visiting this time of evening?" Her disappointment was obvious as they slowly moved along. Mary's recollections of the two—*Jenny and Ted, arm-in-arm at the top of the walkway*—haunted her; while the evocative spirit of Jenny told her that something was wrong, that her brother was in trouble this evening.

"'*Out visiting?*' That's possible. But I doubt it. Especially if he's leaving tomorrow. *He wouldn't do that.* And Puck's not around, either," he acknowledged his son while warily scanning the bay, peering up through the shadows and trees toward the darkened cabin. Expecting his brother-in-law to shout out his welcome from atop the ropewalk as he always did—*and for an instant, he too could see the young couple striding down to meet them, waving in unison*—he uneasily added, "Let's tie up and unload our gear. We need to get this stuff up the hill or we'll be stumbling around in the dark before long."

It wasn't right: *Ted's boat missing.* In his letter he said he'd leave it; but wet moorings and ramps, and oil-and-gas slicks visible around the floating dock showed that others were ahead of them, *and only shortly before.*

"He must have left earlier. It's not like him to be on the lake this time of evening. *Where would he go?*" Mary puzzled while peering past the bay's perimeter, past its out-buildings, the smokehouse and wood pile, and past the bear-proof ice house set into the trees and now used only for wood storage; then out over the darkened water...

"He wasn't at Gus's, unless we missed him going the other way. But I don't believe—"

"We didn't miss him," Jeremy insisted. "We never saw *anyone* pass us. We're practically the only ones out here."

Jeremy was right. And her father agreed. Since leaving Walkers Landing, they saw no one except that *one lone fisherman* at the entrance to the narrows.

"He could have gone through the ranger station," Mary offered. The ranger station was east of Ted's, on the south shore of Kabetogema, and on the north end of the narrows, so her suggestion made sense despite being late in the day.

"That's possible. So where does he board the bus? It doesn't stop at the station, you know. It doesn't run that far. And why were *two* boats tied here? And not very long ago, either," Owen pointed to the evidence.

"Was it one of the rangers, maybe?" Jeremy tried again. *"They* could have taken him to the bus."

"—Or someone to pick up the dog? Someone had to take care of Puck, you know," Mary argued, knowing well that Ted often took Puck to Alma Halsey's when he planned to be gone for long.

"Puck doesn't need 'taking care of'—"

"No," she persisted, "but you know Ted couldn't just *leave* him here."

"No, I suppose not. Sure."

But Owen was no more convinced of plan changes than were his wife and daughter. *Not at this hour.* Not with the sun soon to set. And not with the weather about to act up. Besides, Ted would have somehow called to report those changes. Or he'd have *at least* let the Klostermans know on his way through. But lacking a better answer, and with darkness nearly upon them, unloading the boat and preparing the cabin for the night remained their first order of business.

After securing their craft, paying special attention to tying up tightly for the night because the wind was predicted to increase, Owen began hauling heavier boxes and bags up the suspended walkway. The *walkway* was a kind of cross-cleated wooden path that bounced and strained against its rope supports, the sway and steepness and the chance-of-slip making the bridgeway hazardous and taxing for city sidewalkers. Then while catching his breath, he set about filling and adjusting the gas lanterns in the screened-in entryway before all daylight was lost. For heating and cooking and for his refrigerator, Ted used propane fuel hauled to the cabin in fifty pound tanks. But for lighting, white gas proved best, although many residents were turning to battery and solar where power lines were unavailable. Meanwhile, with Dusty trailing close behind, Keith and Jeremy carried up smaller articles as their mother busied herself with unpacking bags and putting supplies away.

On one trip down the path, Owen noticed a freshly-smoked cigarette butt at the edge of the water and an empty whisky bottle in the grass nearby; while on another, Jeremy retrieved a well-worn but untarnished jack knife beside the trail, a curiosity her parents couldn't explain, but cause enough to redress the notion that something was amiss and that Ted tried leaving a message.

Storing perishables in Ted's gas-run refrigerator, and dry goods and clothes in the many built-in cupboards and closets around her, Mary searched and fretted for the right spot for each. "He's got every nook-and-cranny filled with things he'll never use," she complained. "He's even got some of Nancy's old clothes stashed away in here." Then taking in Ted's familiar surroundings, she wondered aloud at what cigarette ashes were doing on the table, reflecting that "this place isn't as neat as it should be—at least, not for Ted. Look at the coffee cups," she puzzled. It was out of character for him to leave his home in such disarray, unless something called him away in a hurry. "And the coffee pot is still warm," she added. But if he was called away, she knew that a note would be left, or a message, *or a trail of bread crumbs*, or…*whose knife had Jeremy found? And who was smoking cigarettes in Ted's cabin?*

Aware of her concern, Owen asked from the porch, "Ted doesn't smoke, does he?" He knew the answer but felt his wife's need for conversation, some sort of reaction, anything to get her mind off the mystery.

"Not since Jenny died," she testified to Jenny's intolerance of his old habit. Jenny's zeal for neatness rubbed off on her brother, so the scattering of messes about the kitchen had to be signals, perhaps clues to his safety.

Owen was about to add something; but just then, from the back porch where he was working with the lanterns, he was startled by a crimson inboard darting through the dusk on its way toward the narrows from which they had just emerged. A strange sight in these waters, he knew no local guide or fisherman would find practical the low-slung design of *that* craft as he watched it careen through the choppy waves, especially with darkness and windy weather bearing down on them. Out of place, it added an uneasiness to Ted's absence.

Finally settled in after an impromptu supper of hamburgers and baked beans along with a freshly prepared lettuce salad Ted left behind, the dishes were washed and put away. It appeared that Ted left for the cities a day earlier than planned, although circumstances surrounding his departure remained clouded and required investigating. At the very least, a trip to the ranger station tomorrow was in order, *and Ted would need some talking to.*

While Mary read by the yellow-white glow of a Coleman lantern, with Dusty sleeping at her side, Keith and Jeremy watched their father experiment at the controls of Ted's battery-powered radiophone, a powerful rig used by a handful of area coast watchers. Owen had no intention of contacting the station—*not at this hour,* and not even with Ted's awkward absence. But he turned the set on anyway and, surprisingly, traffic was heard: "Dixon on North Namakan...Wilson party located...." Static followed, with a reply, "O.K., Dwight, thanks for the help." Then a more distant voice crackled the air, "Rangers, this is Smitty at the falls...copy the Wilson report. We got the same news from the Canadian side." More static and another reply, "Right, Smitty. Catch you tomorrow, and...you say hello to your family."

Finally, it was quiet, ten o'clock, and well past check-in time for the lake's reporting stations, so the next transmission came as a bold surprise, for instead of the static-impregnated voices of far-off and impersonal communications, there cut through the airways a clear and frigid report:

"*Unit two...anything show?*"

"Not yet. And it's getting rough out here. The wind's up some more, and it's too dark to do any good tonight."

"Unit two...*location?*"

"We're fifteen minutes west of Walkers, and no sign of him. You might have Wayne of Johnny check Big Timber if he went that far."

"Right...*you got that Johnny?*"

A weaker, static-filled response: "We're headed there now...go to alternate."

A frown etched Owen's face long after communications stopped.

"Is something wrong, Dad?" Jeremy worried.

"No. Nothing's wrong, honey," he insisted.

But something *was* amiss. *Something was very wrong.* Feeling apart, he was unable to confirm his fear that the trouble might involve Ted. Running upriver to Big Timber was a long shot this time of night, and in open water, at that. He couldn't believe Ted would head there. For what reason would he go that way, or that the rangers would even investigate? *Why would they do that?* But without cause for a disturbance just now, he resolved to wait until morning before revealing this new concern to his family.

Forcing a smile, he turned to his on-lookers and announced, "Time for bed."

It was agreed that Jeremy would sleep on the down-filled couch in the living area while Keith got the army cot that he knew his uncle stored under the back steps along with his fishing equipment and life jackets and the berry buckets everyone added to over the summers. He long-ago planned to top the cot with an air mattress and a sleeping bag and to move it to the screened-in porch overlooking the lake's dock area. From there he could see the stars and hear the wind (The wind had picked up since sundown) hushing through the pine and poplar without having to worry about nighttime intruders. Once settled, Owen turned down the lamps, and before long, everyone, including Dusty, was asleep.

It might have been an hour, maybe two. Keith could not be sure. But through the whistling of the wind in the trees and above the distant, lonely howling of Timber Wolves, he was awakened by what he thought was the idling of a boat motor, then...*voices?* It couldn't be—*not out here.* Listening closer, he now heard nothing but the lapping of waves on the floats of the dock below. Perhaps it was only a dream, or...the wind, or...it didn't matter as he drifted off to sleep once more.

The next morning, over bacon, eggs, and wild rice, Keith reported what he thought he'd heard last night. His mother smiled and Jeremy teased; but his father remained steadfast, not sharing in the taunts and looks of skepticism when, indeed, the *looks* and *taunts* were suddenly interrupted by Dusty's barking and by the hollow thump of boots coming up the back steps.

To their amazement, they knew the tired-looking and disheveled gentleman who stood at the back door to greet them, along with two smiling forest rangers.

Chapter 7

"I'll swing by the place on my way to Halsey's," Ted reported over his radio. "I'll probably make her bay around…say…*noon* tomorrow," he calculated, "if the weather's not too rough," he relayed his concern to the ranger. "Otherwise it might have to wait."

Although over-trusting with people, Ted was careful with the weather and water and whims of nature. Tall and lean, he was stronger and more resourceful than he looked. Framing his piercing eyes and narrow nose, his face was clean-shaven and thoughtful, but graying and paunched below his jaw line, signs of age he ignored. A sober woodsman, observant and cautious, he contemplated his actions carefully, and was quick to criticize the careless.

"I've got the week's mail, and I promised her some Walleye; and I've got to drop Puck off, anyway. She'll take care of him while I'm gone," he added, wishing he could leave the black Lab with his sister.

It was Wednesday evening, two days before the Petersons' expected arrival, *and two days before his anticipated run to the cities.* The timing was terrible because their paths would cross by only a few hours, and he knew the kids would be disappointed. But his *real* concern was that Percy Greenwall had appeared on the docks again. Ted was uncomfortable with young Greenwall around, the banker's boy slick as snail oil; and it made him re-think his trip to the cities. All the while, Ted forced from his mind the reality, *the impossibility* of what had happened within the Ash River gorge five years ago…that it was during a similar trip, *and for similar reasons,* when Jenny had disappeared.

In spite of Ted's concern, little could be done about Percy. The man was unpredictable, showing up where least expected and spiriting away when spotted. Little could be hidden from him, for Percy had his supporters and sources of information; and he was sufficiently familiar with Currie Island, the place Ted planned to check before his stop at Widow Halsey's, to tie knots in his otherwise rugged reserve.

One year ago, Ted recalled having breakfast at the counter bar at Jenny's bay window of what was now his radio room when he'd witnessed Greenwall's boat emerge from the narrows. It was unusual to see him up and running so early because Percy was a night owl; and his appearance back then had been cause enough to recall that he and the Currie boys were about to strike a deal on Bill Lawman's Big Timber bait shop.

Ted knew the place. He was familiar with Big Timber. And he

knew that young Nels had mixed emotions over the deal because they'd talked about it; and Nels needed all the good advice he could get. The boys didn't know who Percy was but for what they'd heard while growing up, as well as recent warnings from their friends. So Nels was undecided: should they buy the place or not? Should they deal with Percy or leave it alone? Except for what his brother Eddie remembered—*except for his mother's attachment*—Nels came to realize that it was a poor investment and a purchase *Ted* discouraged outright, calling Big Timber a waste of money; *and Nels trusted Ted.* By then, *a year ago,* Bill Lawman had moved to Florida, leaving his old home to the mercy of the elements, at which Percy snatched it up for taxes and a tap dance. Nobody wanted the store; nobody could use the place because utilities hadn't been maintained, nor could a road be built for high water. Ted had warned the boys their real estate man was *banking* on a quick buck. And the Klostermans had warned them, too. In turn, they informed Nels that Percy was known to cheat his clients; and there were others who could testify to Percy's behavior, as well. But the two—*especially Eddie*—had fallen in love with the spot because of what their mother remembered about it, no matter that she and her sons hadn't gone back in months.

A year ago, in spite of the warnings, and despite good advice from friends, Nels had reluctantly sealed the deal, a worrisome decision for Ted, for with Mother Currie gone, Nels and Eddie had become easy prey for scoundrels like young Greenwall.

The early-morning sighting of Percy-at-the-narrows *a year ago* so concerned him that while planning a tour of his pulpwood operation back then, Ted had decided on a quick check of Currie Island.

He remembered, *a year ago,* landing near where remnants of the Currie bathhouse still stood, he'd tied his boat to a rock, then stepped out to look around. His find, if not earth-shattering, was noteworthy, for scattered about had been bits and pieces of a carelessly constructed fire, an improvised lean-to-for-show, and an empty cigarette pack in the grass—*Percy's brand*—and proof-enough that the island had been recently visited. But there'd been nothing more and nothing particularly alarming about his find because others had landed there from time-to-time, fishermen and campers; and even *he* had occasionally stopped by to police and patrol the place.

After reporting his observations *at that time,* Ted shared them with Gus and the Klostermans because Percy's activities, outrageous as they could be, were Neal's right to know—*and a word of warning for Gus.* They were one big family on the river, so *everyone* had a right to know.

But despite that closeness, Gus remained obstinate, a thorn in the foot of their *one family* because of his lack of malice toward *anything* that was *Greenwall.* Within juxtaposed loyalties, Gus was a picture of cooperation and support to Ted and neighbors. *He was a good man,* a friend to the unfortunate and appreciated by every honest soul who knew him. But when patching up differences with his step-daughter, he was another person, a supporter of

Percy Greenwall. That ambivalence and sometimes sightless trust in the wrong people drove his friends to frustration. But the real paradox, and the aggravation it generated, was that Gus's disposition fit the temperament of Ted Snelling, himself.

Current briefs had some of the ransom money turning up at Big Timber a few days earlier, found under a mattress at the ramshacklement Percy sold them a year ago. Then *someone* saw the boys in a Berry Falls tavern a few days later, *spending money they didn't have*, although *most* realized the boys' aversion to the inside of a pub, doubting they were alive at all.

For now, Ted had two problems: Big Timber was near his home and needed to be checked. But watching the north end, Bill Lawman's old spot, was difficult because it was hidden by a bend in the channel, the whole isthmus up the lake from his patrol. To satisfy apprehensions over what Percy might have done with the boys, Ted relied on his friend and coast watcher near Pine Island to keep tabs at Lawman's.

Unfortunately, the Currie home near Kettle Falls, in the *opposite* direction, was *equally* inaccessible, *equally* worrisome. The boys grew up there, *down the lake,* and on no beaten path: few visited that remote island. Mindful of this, and because his own cabin was the closest station to the old homestead, Ted volunteered to inspect Currie Island as a favor to authorities who were equally skeptical of new sightings there.

"O.K., Ted," Whitcomb's voice crackled over the radio. "You leave day after tomorrow, right?" Because of the open radio link, Ted's travel plans were no secret.

"That's right, Charlie. I figure to catch the bus from Gus's...."

Ted was agitated. He was nervous. Everyone on the lake knew he was leaving for the cities. Unfortunately, everyone *also* knew that his sister's family was arriving the afternoon of his departure, and having the likes of Greenwall around while they were here did not set well with him. Ted understood Percy's deceptiveness, and Mary did too; but she and Owen had no way of knowing that his sinister side had ruptured wide; they had no way of comprehending that he was out of control.

"Hope it works out," the ranger returned. "I won't have the evening watch tomorrow. Earl's on for a couple days; and before I forget, the weather for tomorrow...rain ending mid-day with north-west winds increasing through evening hours," he parroted a wire-copy weather summary fed hourly through the ranger station.

"Thanks a lot, Charlie. We'll look out. Anything else to pass along?" Charlie Whitcomb had nothing more, so Ted signed off. Then, just as he did nearly every evening since his wife died five years ago, he waited a moment before pressing the mic button again. Solemnly, he added, *"Good night, Jenny."*

The next morning, *Thursday morning,* dawned wet and dreary, with the predicted cold front covering most of northern Minnesota. But the anticipated wind had not yet materialized; so as Puck paced the dock, watching for the "get up, boy" signal,

Ted loaded supplies and filled a cooler with walleye for Widow Halsey. Then packing rain garb, and with Mrs. Halsey's mail sealed safe and dry within a plastic storm pouch, he set out for Indian Point, a remote island off Kabetogema's north shore. Widow Halsey, one of the original north shore leaseholders, lived alone, her children grown, her husband passed away. Without family nearby, and now in her eighties, she relied on area residents for mail, staples, and assistance; and on this trip she agreed to return Ted's many favors by caring for Puck. The retriever was a good dog and gentle, but uncomfortable with strangers; so Ted needed a familiar face while he was away, and Mrs. Halsey fit the bill.

On his way across, with Puck perched at the bow of his boat, riding the waves like a reckless horse jockey, his ears flapping carelessly in the wind, Ted detoured down the Namakan channel toward an expanse of islands marking the boundary waters' turn toward Kettle Falls, a Canadian landmark with a scandalous and colorful past.

At the falls, a wooden, two-story hotel had been constructed in 1913 by a timber man named Ed Rose or by another (It's been argued) named W.E. Rodie (perhaps the same man), and financed by Madame Nellie Bly, but not to be confused with the investigative journalist, Elizabeth Jane Cochrane, who adopted that name. In 1918 Robert Williams bought the hotel for a thousand dollars and four barrels of whisky from the Madam; and with the Williams family in charge, therein grew a tradition of home cooking and hospitality; then in 1987 the hotel was renovated and subsequently run by the Park Service. Uniquely, the boundary between the United States and Canada runs through Kettle Falls Dam, allowing visitors to stand on U.S. soil and look south into Canada.

But the islands Ted was approaching were west and south of this landmark within a complicated maze of outcrops and the sight of frequent search efforts, and it was no place for unproven outsiders to be exploring. Some of the larger islands in the southern part of the channel include Namakan, Round Bear, Williams, Kubel and Cemetery; while others like Fox Island, Moose Island, Blue Island, and Squirrel Island are nearer the falls. There is also Blind Island Narrows, Sheen Point, Tar Point, and Old Dutch Bay. The islands are wooded and pristine, so newcomers and the inexperienced often find difficulty determining their size and shape or in judging the main shoreline from what is not. As many tenderfoots discover, even with sophisticated GPS devices, and electronic compasses, this is an excellent place to get lost. But for those who know the lay, it is an ideal escape. Ted realized that few understood this region as well as did the young fugitives, although it was unlikely they would return to their crime scene or risk being discovered at all.

As Ted approached, thoughts of an earlier time entered his mind: with acquaintances west of Kettle Falls and friends on Sexton Bay, he and Jenny would pass this way; and it was then that they grew close and one-of-mind. But even before he met her, even before the small island became Currie Island, mom and dad

Currie spent summers there with their boys, the innocent days when Ted would laugh with pride at being called "Uncle Ted" by two youngsters indelibly drawn to the land. The Curries were old friends by then, rugged and durable, and the boys—*especially after their father died*—had become a permanent part of his life.

Currie Island was among the first and smallest in the group marking the turn into Canada along the route traveled by the Voyageurs of old; and he felt the isolation *they* must have felt as he found himself center-pieced within his timeless cross-section of nature, timbered and untouched. If not for his garb and the machinery that propelled him along the water, *he* might have come from the world of the Voyageurs and been magically dropped into the present, because Currie Island—*all the islands*—had changed little from that time. Friendly and serene, the old place—*the Currie place*—presented no more reason for trouble than when the gray-eyed lobo ran the land.

But as the island—*Currie Island*—stood out from the rest, *it was apparent that not all was well on Namakan Lake, for like a rogue thunderbolt piercing the calm of an evening's gentle rain, unexpected and foreign, a gunshot broke the silence!* Ted looked about to see from where the shot came—then *two more* were heard in quick succession, their harsh reports blending and echoing in rolling undulations down the channel. *Crack! Crack!* he listened; then *c-r-ak...c-r-ak!* came their echoes, intrusive and alien. Someone clearly intended to shatter the calm, to attract attention, the timing so contrived that Ted expected it to happen again, and was disappointed when it did not.

Cutting his speed, Ted was determined to avoid conflict, for he had no desire to get shot at like his ranger friends had last summer. With caution urging him home, even as common sense told him to leave the area, a dated outboard with a powerful motor *like the one the Currie boys owned* darted from a rock-walled enclave on the island's lee side where the Currie cabin once stood, then quartered away, back toward the narrows and toward his own small bay seven miles distant.

Ted realized the *escape* was staged. *He knew it was.* And he realized the *escapees* were on the radio this morning awaiting his arrival, then outstripping him to remain unidentified, with only the boat presenting a convenient clue to whom it was. And he knew what he would find with *another* examination of the island: a crude, lean-to shelter and the smudged remnants of *another* fire, *like the one last year,* used neither for cooking nor warmth. But now, with nothing to prove and little to gain by a further search, he reported the incident by radio, then turned about to complete his trip to Lost Lake and his visit with Widow Halsey.

Finally reaching his cabin, Ted was alone and lonely without his dog. It was late afternoon, the western-horizon clouds breaking up, and the rain having stopped earlier in the day. He'd packed his bags in anticipation of his trip to the landing tomorrow, the bus due in before breakfast; so he and his *ride* would have to leave early. Looking forward to a light supper and an early retirement, he wasn't interested in company or complications. But it was increasingly windy as he arrived, so he wasn't surprised to find another boat tied to his dock. This was common in northern waters with sudden changes in the weather. He could remember accommodating travelers forced off the lake by a squall or freak storm and even by a white-out one early-winter. And he recalled his own reliance on the hospitality of neighbors because the open water could turn suddenly mean. No...a strange boat wasn't unusual. But he *was* surprised to find *that same craft* he saw darting from Currie Island only hours earlier, *the same one he saw after the decoy shots were fired.* Incredibly, this raised no hackles of caution. After all, it wasn't Percy's boat. *It was the boys' boat.* And even if Percy *was* running it, his social call should carry no evil intent.

Or should it?

Ted wondered if Percy knew the purpose of his trip tomorrow...that *he* was the target of a fact-finding commission, an uneasiness now stealing his thoughts. *He and his investigator friends were too careful to reveal any secrets!* He'd had minimal correspondence with Saint Paul...no unnecessary talk...nothing to compromise the investigation. So...*no way* could Percy know, *unless one of the justice people got careless.*

Unfortunately, underestimating Percy's *sources* was only part of Ted's problem. More critically was his inability to fathom Percy's jealousies, the effects of his conversations with Roxanne. He hardly intended to compete for her—*certainly not for Roxanne.* His discussions with her were for guidance and advice and...*what harm was there in that? Roxanne could use the advice.* And it was proper counsel, given the forgotten scandal, *that Uncle Cyrus was likely her father.* Roxanne was probably his own cousin! *Had Mary or Gus thought of that!* But even if she *wasn't* family, he ignored the notion that Roxy and Percy had joined forces. He drove from his mind her well-known *attitude* toward the Snellings and toward her stepfather, or that she'd fallen to an even *deeper* low. If Percy's pride was chaffed, it escaped Ted that *she* may be the cause for his presence this afternoon...that *she* had pointed Percy up the river, or that *she* had a hand in Jenny's death.

For Ted, that was impossible.

But the *real* impossibility—*the dilemma his friends must contend with*—was how the old woodsman's trust and confidence in the wrong people could be so frequently and incredible placed.

Ted trusted everyone. In the wilderness, where cooperation was often key to survival, Percy and Roxanne's bad behavior was overlooked. Like Gus, the country's purity programmed him into believing that chivalry prevailed, that the good in everyone *always* outweighed the bad.

Perhaps it did. *In the long run.*

But for the moment, the bad in Percy was wreaking havoc with Ted's honor system, for when he opened the *always-unlocked* back door to his cabin, he found Percy sitting there like an exhausted frog at the dinner table, a grim-fit smile on his mottled face, a gun in one hand, and a cigarette in the other. In fact, he presented a laughable-enough picture, if not for the short fuse Ted imagined burning under his backside.

"Hello, Ted," a sandpaper catch in his voice.

Without Puck to back him up, Ted was a stranger in his own

home. He could do little but close the door behind and reply, "Hello, Percy. I didn't know that boat was yours. Weren't you running it down the channel this morning? Weren't you at the island? *Did you buy it from Nels?*" he prodded. "How much did you give him for it?" He jabbed again.

Aside from the obvious barbs, he offered no real reprimand, no arguments, and few questions. Ted didn't challenge his guest for showing up the way he did, smoking like a riverboat stack; and he said nothing of his threatening posture this evening, for even with his gun-in-hand, Percy was welcomed. And he didn't ask about the Currie boys, either. With Percy's appearance in the brothers' boat, he could piece together their fate, as well as the fate of that unlucky attorney a couple summers ago. But still in denial over his role in Jenny's death, Ted settled on *where* and *how* Percy found out about his Saint Paul meeting, although he could guess at that, too.

"You were on the radio, weren't you," he concluded. Radio frequencies were shared on the lake, common needs making privacy impractical, with everyone's affairs, like locker-room convenience, becoming public knowledge.

"That's right," his guest easily nodded, a ring of cigarette haze encircling him like an errant halo, or like the malevolent thunder cloud that hung over some dark and maligned few.

Older and heavier than he remembered, and apparently a good deal slower, too, Percy's red, waxened complexion presented a clownish sight which misrepresented the area's lean mold; and as he sat hunched over, smoking and looking drawn, Ted was tempted to chide him about his health and weight and poorly disguised drinking habit. Instead, he asked:

"What tipped you off, Percy?" Ted knew that monitoring radio conversations might have provided his timetable for the next few days, but there was nothing in those confabulations to disclose his trip's *real* purpose, and nothing to implicate Percy, himself.

Mildly surprised, Percy revealed, "Well, *the kid.*"

"What do you mean, 'the kid'?"

"Well, *sure*, the kid. He's been watching the mail room for me. You couldn't figure that out for yourself? Some sleuth *you* are," a staccato-like chuckle, his taught smile grimmer than ever, like the mad Cheshire in Alice in Wonderland.

His voice, gravely-soft and high-pitched, fell short of his ruddy appearance, a vintage cartoon character waxing and waning with moves and gestures. Like his father, he was a big man; but *unlike* him, his disregard for personal appearance painted him paunchy, the bulbous bad guy in some old flick Ted had seen, ill-fitted suit and all. For Percy, his admission about Freddie's eavesdropping was true enough, and a point of pride that Ted had not caught wind of Freddie's deeds. But he labored to hide his resentment at being bested for Jenny, as well as his ludicrous impression that he was *now* being challenged for Roxanne. He was disappointed with Ted for his lack of understanding, as if his festering hatred for the Snellings had been wasted all these years or, *worse yet,* that Ted hadn't realized his simmering odium, or wasn't at all attracted to Roxanne.

Holding *that* inside, the best he could muster was a fleeting, pouting look of irritation that Ted completely missed.

Instead, Ted said, *"Gus's hired boy?* Freddie? You're using him, Percy. That isn't right."

"'Isn't right?' What do I care if—"

"Don't you realize what he's gone through? That kid's had some bad luck," he sermoned. "He's got enough on his plate without you adding to it," a purposely shallow string, for he knew his monologue had no affect. "If you want to help," he continued, "let Gus take care of things. *He* knows what to do."

"'Gus'? Hah Gus don't know nothing—"

"Gus has seen *plenty* of kids like Freddie come through. What you're doing will just mess it up for him," Ted hardened, at which Percy looked bored and about to implode; but as he started to defend himself, he realized Ted was not his typical audience, so he merely nodded, an ominous lack of concern: *why should he care about Freddie?* Using him was crucial to his plans.

After a pause, each calculating the other's resolve, Ted asked, "Now what do we do?" With Freddie likely aware of Percy's agenda, Ted was convinced the young man was in danger, assuming *that* detail hadn't already been settled.

Regrettably, it was Ted who missed details: with Jenny's death, he might have better reacted to Percy and Roxanne, *each* malcontent on separate tracks, but *each* with agendas leading to Gus's property. *Everyone else* saw it…what went on under Ted's nose—*under Gus's nose.* Apparently, *even Freddie figured it out.* Jenny would have been furious, her growing conviction that Gus's assets had been the pair's target all along, *the very concern that likely nudged Percy toward his final vengeance on her.*

Gus's assets....

Gus Walkinen's assets included his local digs, as well as four miles of Gray Lake shoreline his family had laid claim to for seventy years. His was the last significant private parcel bordering the park, a choice piece, and Percy's goal. From what Ida surmised, half this strip was Roxy's *if she could maintain favor with Gus.* But maintaining favor was impossible for her: *everything* was done *the hard way.* And so it was...with Freddie's unwitting assistance and with Gus crazy-glued to Percy like a future father-in-law, the two swindlers, each with their own agendas, stood a fair chance of winning it all.

When Neal and Becky saw Greenwall slide toward Walkers like a Machiavellian claim jumper, they'd suspected the worst, and expressed their fears with Gus. But the old landowner was too trusting to believe any of it. Although a good judge of character, he'd *always* been deluded by Zita's daughter...serious miscalculations, although understandable errors of a devoted father.

Freddie's involvement was less sinister but more pivotal than most realized. As Percy's inside man, his motives were likely friendship or the promise of reward—*or simple naiveté.* With access to the mailroom, he supplied Percy with Ted's itinerary. On one occasion, after Gus sorted the evening truck and went to bed, Freddie entered the post office with a key he'd made and stumbled upon a *packet* from an *agency* in the cities; and although addressed to Ted Snelling, it contained news of great interest to Percy Greenwall.

"Now what, Percy? Do we just sit around here and wait?"

His antagonist shrugged, "You talked to the widow about what happened this morning? You told her about the gunshots? *The boat?*" He knew she'd spread the word. She *said* she hated her radio, but Percy knew she was on the air the moment Ted was out of sight.

Ted thought for a moment—*he pretended to*—then said, "That wasn't the boys at the island, was it. No, *that was you*," he patronized, for they both knew who was *at the island*. Then he admitted, "Sure, I told her. I told her about *everything*. And I made a radio report, too. But *you knew that.*"

"Good," Percy grumped, pleased with himself. *A job well done.*

"And I'll report it again, tonight."

Ted realized Percy's only concern was in drawing attention to the Currie boys, *as if they were still alive.* Convinced he would share their fate, Ted was in no hurry to join them. Besides, he owed it to Jenny, and he owed it to Neal and to himself to find out what *really* happened to her; and he couldn't do that if he was dead. *Some* of Ted's neighbors toyed with the notion that the Curries had dispatched the attorney, although *most* realized they were incapable of such misbehavior; but Percy also knew how little it took to resurrect a rumor.

"We'll make sure of that. Then biting his lower lip, Percy

added, "I wish you weren't so damned snoopy. *I liked you*, Ted," a quieted lie, as if convincing himself of an impossibility. "I've *always* liked you," this ludicrousness making Ted grimace. He knew Percy needed to rationalize his actions, as if his crimes were for protection rather than greed. "But you couldn't keep your nose clean, could you. Huh?" *This* contradiction made Ted smile, but only grimly. "You had to mix it up with the Feds, didn't you. You had to give advice where it wasn't wanted," he complained. "You had to get Gus all riled—"

Percy held up, at which Ted belayed even *his own grim smile*, only *now* realizing Roxanne's pivotal role, that keeping her and Gus happy was crucial.

"I've Got *deals* brewing with these lake people," he sneered anew. "Got too much to lose with your pokin' 'round an' attorney-talkin'; an' I gotta stop your get-together tomorrow or it all goes *south*. As long as people *believe* the boys are kickin', I'm clear," Percy continued his discourse within himself.

"So if anything goes wrong—"

"'*Wrong*'?" Taken aback at first, Percy then understood: *"That's right! Hah!* If anything goes '*wrong*', if anyone' turns up missin' 'round here, the brothers get blamed," his chuckle broke into a triumphant cigarette cough. "I'll make sure of that," he hacked again, *"an' now you know too much,"* he wheezed, his face redder than ever, his intentions ominously clear. Ted realized that *wherever* the Currie boys rested, he'd soon be joining them, *and he'd likely be joining Jenny, as well.*

"So you faked the smoke and gunshots and phony reports,"

Ted charged, realizing that Neal's missing canoe and stolen staples last fall were stage props for a few fools. Considering Percy's girth, Ted considered chiding him about the missing ice-cream bars; and if he'd been in better humor, he'd have asked about the attorney, *the real story*, and the ransom money, too. But he didn't want to know anymore. *He didn't care.* The thought of Percy's role in the death of Jenny began to marble his passions, to make him angry. And it was an alien feeling for this old woodsman, with anger having little room on his list of emotions.

"Cops figure the Curries were in the cities last week, *damn fools!* Even Roxy doesn't know 'bout that," his eyes flashed wickedly, as if plans for her were still being explored. "And I hear they been setting up roadblocks. *Heh-heh-heh,*" he laughed. "Got 'em runnin' 'round like fat monkeys in a lion's cage," he chuckled again, humored by his own simplistic analogy, a lisping stutter that sounded like the faulty bilge pump in Klostermans' root cellar the day after a rain storm.

Even Roxy doesn't know struck hard with Ted. Pondering Percy's plans for a moment, he asked, "But when they discover the boys are dead, they'll know you cheated them, and—*they're dead,* aren't they, Percy?"

"Yeah, yeah!" Percy tried to snarl. *"They're dead,* all right. *Ain't that obvious?* An' whose fault is *that?* They wanted their money back. How the hell could I give their money back? *I spent it."* He crescendoed, a hollow appeal, as if Ted should be sympathetic, as if Percy's deeds could be justified or magically erased...*as if Jenny somehow deserved to die*...and Ted darkened.

"The authorities will put it together—"

"Oh, *sure*, like *you* 'put it together', I s'pose. It'll take a long time before *they* put *anything* together." Considering Freddie's performance, Ted feared he might be right. "By then I'll have Walkers in my pocket, *me an' the misses,*" he cracked disdain, his cold disregard for those around him making Ted shudder. Getting away with murder was too easy, too convenient for this cynic whose size and appetite outpaced his integrity.

Reaching for something to work with, Ted pressed, "But people are aware—"

"No, Mister Snelling, *they're not 'aware' at all.* They're not aware of *nothin'! I'd* be caught by now—*I'd be in jail by now* if they were so damned 'aware'. Hah! *'Aware'?* I suppose *you* were 'aware', huh? I suppose *you* had it figured out," he challenged.

Ted's concern for himself and for Freddie was real, but it was overshadowed by his family's arrival. "I have people coming...," he started. Warning them was impossible, but he was unsure of how to approach his wheezing adversary, or *the worst scenario:* what this twisted tyrant's intentions were for them all.

But Percy knew about the Petersons.

Everyone on the lake knew when they were arriving. At least they *thought* they knew. "You do what I say an' your in-laws will be safe enough. We'll be long gone before *they* show up."

In return for Percy's ragged promise of security, Ted knew his evening radio report would be critically monitored, his departure for the cities tomorrow, *if it happened at all,* would be a carefully guarded event, and his impromptu partnership with his captor could end at any moment.

Chapter 8

Alma Halsey, silver curled and frail, stepped through the doorway of her manicured cabin of log and stone that she and Jalmer build sixty years ago; then, with the crook of her hand, she shaded her eyes and glasses from drops of cold rain falling since midnight and looked out over the water into a kaleidoscope of colors, like light through rough-cut glass strewn carelessly about. The wind had yet to pick up, but within her private conversations she agreed that it would, for she could see it in the exchange among the birds and in their tenuous float from branch to branch, and in the tips of the trees, their fragile movements undecided, and in the lake's uneven wash upon the shore. Then just as she'd done most mornings, she recounted the quiet serenity and quality of her hermit-like life over the past three score and more. She and Jalmer, who was a trapper by trade when the practice was acceptable and legal, knew no other way, their parents coming from the Finnish countryside a hundred years ago. They were of the Jarvinen and the Halsinen stock, and she was still a Halsinen and was now known as Widow Halsey only by popularity.

She saw people come and go: she had two sons and two daughters, and they all left; she had neighbors, although but few, and they all left; and she had a husband who died so many years past that her memories no longer brought tears to her eyes. She *did* remember (she brightened at this) his physical charm and character, *and how he could fight for what he thought was right!* And the talk of Normandy where in the confusion he was left for dead, *and found again;* and his constant and protracted political battles with every city hall in the county, and every county seat in the state, and even Saint Paul in later years; and as she looked about, his ideas of freedom were closing fast, for they had seen government regulations and prejudices wax and wane and wax again while people's hopes and aspirations were sidestepped or trod upon or ignored completely when failing to speak out.

Years ago, the woods and water was God's domain, and Jalmer used to call it his church and sanctuary, a serious but much too solemn claim for such a stubborn old coyote, she chuckled. *But still a retreat,* she pursed her lips in determination, no matter that wealthy Washingtonians turned it a hideout for their fair-weather friends who would curl up by the fire like spoiled tomcats when the snow began to blow.

She frowned at this, for *they* didn't belong here; then she held in contemplation as she shuffled along: wasn't this land *His* land to share with those who would protect it? To *really* protect it? And wouldn't it remain so long after the rich and fair-weather *adventurers* headed home and snuggled up in bed, she frowned some more; and if she could bring herself to curse those foolish lawmakers, she would.

Perhaps she was growing too old to understand. Or the country was simply growing up around her, forgetting and leaving her kind behind. *I'm still here,* she felt like shouting out, knowing it would do little good. In her mind, a *wilderness of the ages* turned into a public promenade was alien and foolish. Then she sighed, long and drawn-out, for she realized that the changes being made were as inevitable as the seasons, and as sure to come about as she was to die.

But it was nevertheless a disappointment, for there was no rush that she could see into this world. It wasn't overrun with outsiders willing to weather the harsh winters and solitude. *None of that.* The land was too far removed for softened city folk to commute, and it wouldn't be getting any better *despite the litany of benefits the politicians spread about,* she pursed her lips again. Instead of protecting the country and preserving its beauty, the new park promoted taxes and businesses and resort owners and dock-side stores and polished facilities for those who had no intention of staying beyond their week away from work. The whole of northern Minnesota, with its impenetrable lakes and forests, and because of its very vastness, would always be unknown to most; but with the changes, the fringes were condemned to a reservations-only playground for the affluent who, with their fast boats and snowmobiles, would foolishly believe that *they* were some sort of *voyageurs* or *explorers.*

After taking in some minutes of morning air while slowly making her way toward the water over a worn pathway now slippery with drizzulets of rain, she looked back through the caps of jack pine and spruce outlining her back yard, then out over the unsettled waves framing the front, and she contemplated the accuracy of the forecast on the radio last night and compared it to what she could see in the water and the wind and the sky, and she worried about Ted. She worried about *all* her friends. But Ted was special, for within the depth of her blue eyes, she understood an even deeper danger for him, and a more sinister cause for concern than from any storm he might encounter. When he would arrive this afternoon, she would have a long talk with him about this; and about young Nels and Eddie; and about the worrisome banker's boy from Chicago; and about Jenny, too. She would warn Ted to be less like herself—*and less like Gus Walkinen, as well*—and more aware of intruders who were not a part of this world and who had no respect for it.

Travel was difficult for her. But she had the radiophone that she only reluctantly accepted, and with this she would contact her south shore neighbors from time-to-time, including Ted and her friends Earl Morris and Charlie Whitcomb at the ranger station. In her latest exchange last evening, she heard that the wind would be picking up this afternoon; and this was a big concern, for Ted planned to come across later in the day to leave his dog with her. He had a meeting in the cities, and his family was coming tomorrow. But they were arriving much too late to take care of his Labrador companion.

She knew Puck, and Puck knew her. She would watch him until Ted's return, although in Puck's mind, *he* would be running the place, she chuckled to herself again. She had raised dogs years ago, and Puck was from a late litter that her Alphie had; so, in a way, Puck's visits were a homecoming, except that Alphie grew old and passed away.

Alma had few visitors, these days. She thought about this as if apart from herself: *who would journey the breadth of Kabetogema to visit her?* she wondered. Sadly, there were few year-rounders left anymore, so Ted's arrival was much anticipated. Besides, he had her weekly mail. And some walleye, too. There might even be letters from her children. But their newsless notes were of little comfort any longer, for *they rarely came themselves,* their words always laced with reasons for her to give up her lease and to move in with them.

But...not as long as she could manage. This was her home, and it would remain so because Jalmer would have done the same.

It was lonely now and difficult for one so old. But she and Jalmer weren't *always* alone...not all these years. There were others who braved the Namakan wild; and except for the far *northers* like herself, there were those who bridged the gap between the cities and the woods, like Gus Walkinen and the Richardsons and the Snelling brothers, and even the Klostermans in their city-styled way. Mixed among them were the elusive trappers and pelt hunters surviving until after the war; and she wryly wondered where the fair-weather adventurers fit in, *if they belonged at all.*

Then there was the celebrated Currie family, a smile replaced her weathered frown.

Who came first? She couldn't remember. But *their* place, *their island,* was north, and more remote than hers. She laughed at this because the Curries called them *city folks* because she and Jalmer lived so much closer to the station than they. *City folks, indeed.* Each week they would get together for supper and cards—*every Saturday night* for fried fish, potato soup and wild rice, unless the weather was bad. There was no way to back out of their visits because there was no way to communicate in those days. They simply showed up, *for better or worse.*

When the children were old enough, elementary school meant the *two-room* at the landing where a husband-wife team named Lenta shared the duty. Because of the distance, the Lentas were foster parents, the kids boarding in and returning home once a month. During the winter there was limited daylight and dangerous travel. The Currie boys never went to high school. *Not even the seventh grade.* But hers did. And she never saw much of them after that, her eyes misted over (was it the rain?), because high school was in Duluth where they stayed with her sister in a big house on a small hill with a manicured lawn in the city overlooking the harbor and the lift bridge and the foreign ships passing through *and a world far removed from home.*

Alma turned and shuffled back on the raised path between her outbuildings and the cabin; and as she watched a pair of yellow-bellied sapsuckers feeding on sap and insects where they punched patterns of holes in the bark of a black spruce tree, she wondered who would fix the leaks in her roof this year. But she knew her worries were needless, for Ted had a crew set to start soon. She remembered when a violent storm swept the channel—*was that in seventy-five?* She struggled to recall when nearly the whole of her shingling was torn away, and her bath house was swept out into the lake where it bobbed around like a raggedy house boat, although it didn't but two days for Ted's team to descend like a swarm of yellow jackets to rebuild and repair it all.

Chapter 9

"*Make it good,*" Percy warned at report time, "and don't forget," he brandished his pearl-handled pistol, "I've heard you jawing with your Boy Scout pals before. I've heard you plenty of times; so, *no tricks!*"

Aside from their school days *challenge* for Jenny Klosterman, then followed by Percy's suspected role in her drowning, Ted and his guest had *nothing* in common; and they *now* shared little but for Percy's cigarette smoke and his fragmented accusations of unfairness, biased and twisted references to his father's banking career and their unscheduled abdication to Chicago. Percy chose to be embarrassed by the move. But no one else in the family was embarrassed, no one else affected like he was. Percy was a teenager when the Greenwalls pulled stakes. But unlike the rest, he allowed their incident with the congressman to fester, then to grow into a full blown resentment of the Snelling family. Cyrus was no longer around, no longer a thorn. But Ted was close by, *the whipping boy by default.* Within Percy's tortured world, Ted was as Snelling as Cyrus had been.

A Snelling? Perhaps so.

But Ted was no Cyrus. Indeed, he was the antithesis of his uncle, a fact that Percy failed to understand.

Roxy shared with Percy *her own* disdain for the Snellings and *her own* aversion for Ted and his sister, but hers arrived on a different wind. Hers was a domestic can with roots in high school; so *hers* had been swirling about for years. No matter that Ted treated Roxanne as family, she lingered over her fractured lineage, preferring to play the displaced person whose fortunes were passed about like a bag of hand-me-downs in a Charles Dickens urchin house. Privately, she dwelt on Cyrus's transgressions, consumed with the notion that a slice of the Snelling property belonged to her. She rarely mentioned this jealousy to Percy, *and never around Gus,* because her right to any inheritance had been long-ago forfeited through bad behavior. She *knew* she was different. *Of course she was different.* But it bothered her that Ted failed to understand; and it irritated her that he, *like Jenny,* remained so miserably forgiving, so contemptuously helpful, and so despicably good.

"What do I tell them?" Ted sat before his radio attempting to look perplexed and to present as pathetically painted a picture as he could. At home on the air, he held little hope in playing dumb, for Percy wasn't blind, nor was he the fool of the party he had once been—*what few parties he's been invited to*. Although introverted, eccentric, and evil, he wasn't stupid.

"*Just what happened over there!*" Percy tried sounding gruff, his bark an impatient yelp, like a Chihuahua unable to snarl up to snuff. "Report the gunshots—*you know what to say. You know damn well what to tell 'em*. And *make it good, or I'll be back!*" he sputtered, an obvious reference to the Petersons' and their impending arrival.

Ted did as he was told, his antagonist holding trump with his family at stake. Besides, he realized Percy was concerned only with refocusing on the Curries and on the perception that *they* had done away with the attorney. For those who knew him, Percy's play was pointless. On the air, Ted was forced to circumvent the truth even as he fell to outlining his morning observations at the island while mixing in routine affairs of the day. Then he finished by adding:

"Owen, my brother-in-law, will check in for me tomorrow, Earl. You've got the weekend watch, right?"

Percy studied him carefully.

"*That's right,*" the ranger replied. "*I'm* stuck out here this time," he laughed. "You have a nice trip," he signed off with no indication that he was aware of Ted's predicament. Percy nodded satisfaction with the performance, convinced that Ted had spirited no clandestine message through.

Ted's radio room once served as Jenny's sewing room and sitting area, a place to ease back and watch the sun go down. It was a neatly decorated cubicle with built-in closets and cupboards and well suited as a lookout on the north side of the cabin, a perfect place from which to observe the lake and the weather as it developed. In one corner was a large day bed and dresser combination, Jenny's idea for those occasions when guests, like the Petersons, would displace them from their own bedroom. Still framed with her blue-laced curtains, the room's most significant feature, aside from the polished pine floors and knotty pine walls reflecting the rest of the cabin's interior, was its large bay window ordered by Jenny when the cabin was built, and which had required a special barge to transport it to their peninsula. This window afforded Ted an unobstructed view of the open waters encircling his *Rocky Point*. Each evening, by force of habit, he used a pair of mounted marine binoculars to scan the shores and the expanse of water from the eastern extremity of his own small bay to just outside the mouth of the narrow gorge marking the termination of Ash River.

His was a routine watch with few reportable problems. Perhaps once a month a careless traveler might run out of gas or collide with one of the submerged shelves unmarked by buoys and would require attention. But *this* evening, *what he viewed through his binoculars and through Jenny's big bay window evoked greater alarm than anything witnessed from here before:*

"Percy!" Ted hissed. *"Take a look at this!"*

"What?" he twisted around. Paranoid, Percy expected a trick; having lived a life of deceit, his reaction was unremarkable.

"It's them!" Ted exclaimed, still peering through his binoculars.

"What do you mean, *'them'*? Who's *'them'*? What are you talking about?" he growled.

"They're a day early—*the Petersons!* They're coming slow—'round the point," he hunched over his heavy marine glasses, puzzled over his family's lack of speed, and why they were arriving a day early at all.

Confronting a wild range of emotions, Ted realized his sister would recognize Percy; and although not likely to know him as the villain he had become, he knew for as mutually frank as they were this evening, Percy couldn't leave him alone with anyone, *especially his own family.* He and his rival had good reason not to be found together, although their common ground hardly brought them to terms.

"If you're lyin'—" Percy snatched the binoculars, tripod and all; but straining his eyes—*as Ted stood back*—toward the large wooden craft just now struggling from the mouth of the narrows a half-mile distant, he mouthed a silent curse, then declared, *"I'll be!* They *are* early. *That miserable kid! Wait 'till I get my hands on him...we've got to get out of here—now!"* he insisted, apparently failing to realize that the Petersons were lumbering along like a loaded hay wagon on a muddy road. Percy's surprise further indicated confusion and close planning, *thwarted plans,* now; but it also told Ted that "...that miserable kid" was alive and well and, *for some reason,* Freddie had not cooperated with Percy in his latest deviltry.

"Where to, Percy? The only way to any landing is past them," Ted pointed, "and we don't dare cross the big water in this wind." He tried to whine but he wasn't used to complaining. "We'd never make it," an anemic acting job he hadn't the power to master.

The weather-warning was Ted's best ruse to continue unraveling Percy's timetable, for he was more anxious to evacuate the cabin than was his antagonist, the wind meaning nothing to a woodmen often facing far worse. But Ted's contrivance had another purpose: it began his assault on Percy's composure and a signaling of their disparity, Ted drawing from his own character and fortitude, with Percy simply losing ground.

"Just get down to the dock!" Percy yipped, an angry shift of his head toward the back entrance. "Where you're goin' it won't make a damn bit of difference," he cursed anew. His control slipping, he gestured threateningly with his pearl-handled pistol, as if a landing should be Ted's *least* concern.

"—and grab your damn bags," he pointed to the suitcases Ted had packed for his trip. "You think I wouldn't notice? *You think I've lost my mind?*"

Ted obeyed, but persisted, "It's getting too late to get anywhere—"

"Keep movin'!" Percy ordered, looking over his shoulder as they descended the pathway. There was no one at his back and nothing left behind, his caution, a suspicion-driven testimonial to his own lack of character and values.

Secretly dropping his knife, Ted led on. But once on the dock, he tried again, "If I'm gone, they'll wonder what my boat's doing here," he pointed. Although worried that Percy had heard his *boat* plans on the air, Ted gambled on Greenwall not knowing that he intended to leave his craft behind, that a neighbor had arranged to take him to Gus's the next morning.

But this fear melted when Percy gave it a moment, then ordered, "Start it up and stick close," he waved his revolver. "And don't forget I can outrun you," he pointed toward his boat...*the boys' boat*. Having to hurry, to exert himself, the heavier man was out of his realm. Ted hoped the strain would continue eroding his judgment.

"We'll have to head east, 'round the point—"

"I'll decide where we go!" Percy was angry because Ted was right. He knew that to remain undetected, their only course was *east* out of his inlet before the Petersons appeared from beyond Rocky Point...*then to wait until darkness overtook them*. Timing was crucial, but it was a race the Petersons were unaware of. And even if they *had* been aware, they were heading into the wind with their small engine and loaded-down craft. Still a quarter-mile distant, it would take them several long minutes to reach Ted's protected dock area.

Without being seen, the unlikely partners gained a concealed inlet outside Ted's bay. Once there, Percy surprised his companion by ordering his boat, *Ted's boat*, filled with rocks; and with the drain cock opened, it was scuttled, *suitcases and all*, even as the Currie boat in which he'd made his run from the island was drawn ashore and hidden.

When Ted questioned him about this, Percy admitted under his breath, "...Gonna have it show up on Walker's doorstep some day...gonna surprise everyone...boys ain't gonna look so good...."

With that, Ted understood the danger Gus was in, *and Freddie, too*. But he hoped that others—*maybe Freddie, himself*—might know Percy's whereabouts tonight; and he realized that the young man, *of all people*, might be his only hope out of his present predicament. But his own hope aside, it was clear that his sister and family were Percy's unwitting hostages, and that he had no way to warn them.

And after that? Percy's plans? Who could tell? Reading the mind of this delusionist who would murder for money was impossible. But one thing *was* apparent to Ted: *Percy's timing was in shambles.* Ted knew that without proper preparation, disposing of him nearby his own cabin could no longer be the game. Discovering his remains—*any evidence of murder*—so close to home would be too heavy an indictment For Percy to overcome.

"Over there," Percy jabbed his gun toward a washout at the far end of the inlet. To Ted's amazement, Percy had hidden *his own boat,* the sleek, red, inboard in which he'd been seen dashing up and down Ash River, within a washed-out overhang protecting it from the wind: Percy was proving to be a formidable and unpredictable thorn. After retrieving his craft, he said, "We'll just stick tight 'till they settle in a bit. We'll just let 'em sit around awhile and wonder why you're not home. That's what we'll do. Then we'll head out, wide open, *right past 'em.* They won't even know it's us," another nervous chuckle, another rasping cough.

And so they waited....

For an uncomfortable, mosquito-ridden twenty minutes, they sat on the damp ground within their woodland enclosure; and with their backs against the trunk of a fallen balsam, Percy muttered oaths of retribution through a haze of cigarette smoke that curled upward and outward like a frustrated angel anxious to catch the breeze and simply float away...while Ted pondered his next move.

Once the sun had fully set and Percy thought it safe to affect a getaway, he ordered Ted into the passenger seat of his craft; then gunning the flashy inboard through the orange dusk and across the bay, skipping and bounding over the waves, they careened past the cabin, around Rocky Point, through the choppy waters of the Kabetogema Narrows, and on toward the narrow Ash River outlet, *and to a destination Ted could only guess at.*

Reflecting on Percy's behavior—*on his being surprised by the Petersons' arrival this evening*—Ted realized Percy had few options: he was unfamiliar with the north shore of Kabetogema; it was getting dark and windy, so avoiding open water was only prudent; and relative security for Percy was Sullivan Bay. So when Ted recommended *avoiding* Sullivan because of its *dangerous entrance*, Percy grabbed at the bait: *prodded by his own pride and in the face of Ted's contrived caution, he resolved to navigate the dangerous pass...*

Of course, *the pass wasn't dangerous.* It wasn't a hazardous run at all. *Not even at this hour.* Most residents had challenged far worse during stormy weather. In fact, the elements were not particularly threatening. But while waiting for the Petersons to settle in, the unpredictable wind *had* switched to a direct bore down the mile-long gorge. With darkness overtaking them and with the cloaking effect of the waves on the submerged shelves complicating their progress, that narrow stretch with its S-shaped throat could be a little tricky. Even during good weather, attention was given to the underwater traps that could split the hull of a small craft, a potential threat to those unfamiliar with the passage. Considering Percy's background, he *should* have been familiar. But to Ted's mix of relief and surprise, his antagonist elected to run wide open at the pass.

"If you're going through at this speed, you better line it up good!" a legitimate warning; but it was also a prod, *another jab*, an affront to Percy's pride in an attempt to guarantee his continued recklessness and all-out speed.

"I know the way!" he shouted across his shoulder while carelessly quartering through the waves as they rounded the point. Oblivious to Ted's finesse, Percy abandoned what caution he could lay claim to, a proud panic sweeping through him, destroying any remnants of the common sense that even a sometimes-woodsman must maintain.

"Down the left side!" Ted waved. *"And cut your speed!"* He continued his assault, for he had little else to bargain with. *"This ain't no straight shot!"* he warned.

"You keep quiet or I'll tie that anchor rope 'round your neck," Percy ordered, his Chihuahua-like voice matching his one-handed dash through the watery gauntlet. As they raced along, Ted could picture Percy with a cigarette carelessly dangling from his lower lip, the image of a playboy winding his way through some Alpine pass, with a young French *sophisticate* with a flowered bonnet by his side....

Obeying his adversary while remaining momentarily quiet, Ted realized that even if Percy *did* know the narrows, he was distraught, out of his element, and ripe for suggestion. So when they reached the spot where the hidden channel turned left, *the very spot where Jenny's boat was found five years ago*, he again hollered:

"*Turn right—quick—or you'll sink us!*"

Ted's shout wasn't premeditated, nor was it an act of bravery. Rather, his *warning* was a kind of release, the culmination of a desperate gambit. *If given time to reflect, he would have paled at the thought of running aground at full speed!* Nevertheless, with nerves taught as banjo wire, Percy involuntarily jerked the wheel to the right, but *too late to realize his mistake!* In the near-darkness, and traveling too fast to see, Percy squandered his last chance in the split second that he might have used to correct his course and save himself.

But...*too late*! Looming high, dark, and imposing, the granite wall of the narrow's far side instantly stood out before them like a primordial trap, as if to say, *"Wrong Way!"*

Percy, shouting a curse as he jumped headlong from the boat, followed Ted into the cold void even as his craft struck the reef; and in the confusion, the pearl handled pistol he once held in power slipped from his grasp and sank into forty feet of water.

As Percy hit the current, Ted struggled through the backwash and the waves; but he gained sense enough to witness the damage, the grinding crunch of fiberglass on rock as the boat slid up onto a submerged shelf, sharp and ragged. Then twisting grotesquely to its side, the doomed craft slipped back into the deep, a gash in its tri-bow signing its fate.

Just then, Percy bobbed to the surface like a lopsided fishing float gasping for air. With a *gash* of his own across his forehead and his arms flailing helplessly about, he bellowed something like, "…Can't swim!" or "…I'm hurt!" Ted couldn't tell which, because it all sounded the same, a generic, gurgling, *save my foolish ass* kind of plea. True to form, Percy carried no life preservers, nothing that made safety-sense. The only object afloat was an empty gas can being blown into the dark and out of reach. Disoriented, injured, and hardly a champion swimmer, Percy was in danger of being blown out of reach, himself.

But gaining his composure, Ted lunged for a shirt collar, hauling the heavier man to the rocky shelf where they stood hip-deep in the wind-churned surf, and from where they managed to clamber onto the boulder-strewn shore.

Upon reaching safety, spent and cold, Ted announced, "Can't stay here, fella…gotta find you some protection."

It was rapidly turning dark, help was unlikely tonight, and they were in big trouble. *On his own* like he'd not been *on his own* in many years, and unable to swim the channel because of the wind and strong current, Ted found himself on the narrows of Ash River opposite the security of his cabin and, ironically, *less than a half-mile from his own kin*. An unfair development, a lesser man might complain; but as Ted detected lamplight through the windows of his cabin, he reasoned through the furor of the moment that his sister and family were safe; and ridding the area of the likes of Percy Greenwall was worth an evening of trouble.

"We can't stay on these rocks," he repeated. "We'll need a fire. We need to get you dried out and out of this wind," he led his exhausted captor into the shelter and safety of the trees.

Thankful he hadn't tied Ted's hands as he had with the Currie boys last year, Percy nodded, his game finished, his very survival depending on the man he planned to destroy.

"What do we do now? Who's going to help us out here?" Percy wondered, unaware that their little saga had been witnessed from the start by his young, curly-haired friend from Walkers Landing.

Chapter 10

Until yesterday, Freddie Moore hadn't met the Petersons; he knew *nothing* of then but for Percy's fabrications; so he knew little of Keith or Jeremy, either. When he discovered them at Klostermans, he missed the Snelling connection or from where they came. Before Ash River, he didn't know Gus and his Summer House or his stepdaughter who rankled nerves with her drunken boyfriends and parties at Skipper's Inn; and he knew nothing of Neal and Rebecca, their restaurant and tavern upriver reminding him of his Aunt Germaine's *Cajun* place in Mississippi, *what little he remembered of it*, but that Becky's accent was the same, drawn out and willowy-like. He never met the Currie brothers, *his heroes because they knew how to hide and get along on their own*, and he knew *nothing* of the local feuds Percy complained about but *was always embroiled in*.

Dock side acquaintances were the wind to Freddie, isolated by *pomp-and-talk* and a bluster by which he was gauged by everyone from Rebecca to the preacher up-road who was more interested in *saving his soul* than being helpful.

Save his soul? Without Gus's tithing, Freddie wondered how *caring* the preacher would be, *or if his following—his song-singing, do-good flock—understood street life at all*. Fearful of *another* separation, he withdrew from discussions of mom and dad or *family talk*, his flamboyancy and dress, *sloppy pants and hat*, covering his insecurity. Still a stranger, Freddie remained wary, a city boy with a good act. Most didn't realize that six months ago he'd suffered *another* breakup, *his parents and their vices again, and a younger brother he'd not seen in five years*. Before his arrival, his anchors were runaways like himself. In this *new* existence, removed from blind alleyways and fleeing from the law, his *friends* were the *few* he had trouble figuring like *Gus and Neal and Becky and Max,* and...not the preacher at all, *and certainly not his flock.*

Many times he was swept up and shuffled from one temporary home to another, his mind and manners prodded at by counselors and teachers and social saviors with self-fulfilling agendas, but who always allowed him to slip through cracks in the system so they could perpetuate their own jobs. There was *plenty* of cracks, and with no one watching very carefully, *slipping* was done whenever he needed a break. After dropping from sight, he'd reappear like loggered driftwood, only to dry out, get prodded at, and *slip* again.

Eventually rescued by a retired alderman, *Maxwell Blankenship,* a visitor to Ash River and one of the many social workers he'd met in the cities, Freddie found himself enrolled in a trade school learning marine engines, then pointed by *his first real friend* toward Walkers Landing and to the purity of a wilderness no corner of his city mind could fathom.

For weeks, Freddie's apprenticeship went untarnished by the *bangers* he'd followed and fought with, his scars and a broken nose as proof. Sometimes bending the truth, he nevertheless worked hard and was accepted by the locals and became Gus's friend. But memories of a fractured home and shattered childhood lingered; and when no one was around, he would retreat to within himself and grow quiet and lonely and frightened....

"...You stay here as long as you want," Gus replied during one of Freddie's low points. Despite his boldness, Freddie was fearful his tenure at Walkers was temporary. Recognizing this, Gus added, "Just be sure your work's done," he harrumphed pretentiously. Then, "How'd *you* like to run this place by yourself?" a less-than-serious offer, but a credible effort to ease Freddie's fears; and the young man would smile, an *impossible* reaction if not for Gus's secret formula.

Unlike the city, there was little on the river to tempt the street-wise young man, and it remained so for months *until Gus's tempestuous step daughter* (Rebecca used *tempestuous*, like bad weather on the coast) *closed in with Percy-in-tow to lend a hand.* At first, Percy held checked, a brakes-applied, eyes-wide-open examination of the young newcomer, his reaction to Freddie reminding Becky of an awestruck child stumbling into a new candy store. But as he and Roxy paused to calculate Freddie's unique position, they gathered the boy's street-stealth—*at least Percy did*—recognizing his potential for turning Gus's head: *perhaps he could be useful later on.*

To concerned residents, the old man appeared unaware of any conspiracy between Percy and Roxanne. This was unremarkable because *there was none.* The two didn't sit down over chicken dinner at the diner to plot Gus's demise. So theirs was an easy secret to keep. *Because there was no secret.* Of course, it was on their individual minds, but the two lacked any hint of cooperation. Except for the drinking part, they hardly got along. Besides, Gus had *always* been aware of Roxy's motivations. *He knew what she was after.* Even if he missed Percy's plans for Freddie, he wasn't *unaware* of Roxanne's designs. He and Zita had raised her through some tumultuous times that left him myopic, *but not blind.* He'd heard the pair arguing most evening before leaving for Ida's, *just like with all her boyfriends.* But unlike the others, Percy promised more grit than the average goldbricker; so Gus was hopeful his daughter would amount to something with Greenwall aboard.

Neighbors could see Gus's nearsightedness: the old landowner would do anything to mend his relationship with her. For them, Percy was a *last-ditch* to that reconciliation, but otherwise relatively harmless. *That's what most saw, and that was no secret.* However, not everyone was convinced:

"*Not if you ask me,*" Nellie Laubquist offered. Nellie, the caretaker of the trailer park's laundromat, knew the boys because they'd stayed there for a time after their mom died. She was a talker and a busybody who never got it right. "If you ask me, them Currie boys aren't around anymore because Percy drowned 'em right after he sold 'em Lawman's place, and he probably did the same for Jenny, and that attorney fella, too."

Of course, nobody asked Nellie. *What could she know?* After all, she *also* thought Percy wrote the ransom note; and they all laughed at this.

Ironically, Percy and Roxy had it all. In his own way, Gus *guaranteed* as much, *but fell just short of putting it on paper.* Despite appearances, Gus's *lovebirds* rarely communicated: Roxy couldn't communicate normally because everything had to be done *her* way...*the difficult way;* and Percy was disenchanted with his bullheaded *Cinderella,* a family flaw most missed. Summarily, Gus was too slow for Percy and too vague for Roxy, his snail-paced plans, *despite good intentions,* squandered by both larcenists in their headlong rush to have it all.

For Roxanne, this urgency transcended simple greed. *She* feared *the old King* might up and die. Or that he'd fall infirmed before the anticipated transfer. It was a fear she'd lose her tenuous inheritance, just as *mom* lost hers years earlier. *Who could blame her? She'd been taught to be afraid.* Percy was equally apprehensive, but *her* worries were more complicated, *her* issues more than mere *money.* Because Gus neglected to adopt her, she felt compromised: nothing recorded—*nothing in print. So, what guarantees did she have?* Gus's was a game of trust she could neither tolerate nor comprehend, its outcome uncertain and potentially empty. She'd even heard rumors that he'd left everything to Mary Peterson since she was the only one Gus knew—*the only one on the river*—who had children he likened to grandkids. Gus was incapable of understanding Roxanne's fears because he loved his daughter; but she remembered that with Cyrus's inconsistencies, her mother's link to the Snelling fortune was severed; because of Grandpa Eb's stubbornness, her ties to the Richardson holdings were never realized; and now, because of Gus's insufferable foot-dragging—*innocent or not*—she might lose claim to the Walkinen wealth, as well.

For Percy, the game was less sophisticated. For him, *everything* was less sophisticated because greed was his only master. *Greed*, and his manifest fancy that *all* the Snellings—*including Ted and his sister*—and *all friends* of the Snellings must pay the forfeit for his father's fall: they were *all* his enemies, an irrationality finding legitimacy within his errant soul.

The Klostermans realized as much and tried warning Gus of the dangers of a Roxy-Percy union. To them, Percy's motivations were clear; but there were also signs from Roxanne. Once she begged title to a lakeside parcel that she squandered for pocket money; then it was funds for patio furniture or something equally frivolous, yet harbingers to her *intentions*, including a *home* where she'd keep Gus under wraps, and to which only *she* held the key. Nevertheless, Gus remained blinded by her smiles and by Percy's friendly face around Freddie; and to the chagrin of their friends, even Ted missed the signals.

Unfortunately, young Freddie lost, too. He knew nothing of the strife *young* Roxanne had created, nor of the clash between Ted's father and his Uncle Cyrus. *He had none of that.* He had merely Percy's plans of retaliation hidden within a guise of good will through which the young street-runner could not see.

Controlling Gus was easy for Percy—*as long as Roxanne occupied his mind;* and putting step-dad away was an option he *also* entertained, but with a less sophisticated formula than Roxy's family plan. Manipulating *the boy* turned equally simple once he'd uncovered some nauseating problems, *Freddie's feelings of rejection, his inadequate friends, an uncaring family, and the obligatory string of heart-to-hearts that Percy reluctantly pursued*....

"...C'mere, son," he beckoned one Sunday evening from near the tool shed where Freddie knew was stored a bottle of *beverage* within a nitch of the low strung rafters, their talks *always* outside or in the shadows where Percy wouldn't be overheard. Freddie resented being called *son* by this red-haired *agent* who reminded him of Pappa Frezno, a restauranteer on Hennepin Avenue. Pappa was a red-faced, mottle-nosed copy of Percy, except Freddie knew first hand that Percy couldn't boil an egg. Pappa made the best deep dish in the cities and Pappa didn't call him son.

It was past supper hour and Freddie was in a hurry because he knew Gus was upset with him for not showing up on time. "I can't talk now," he kept walking. "I can't keep Gus waiting." Surprised by Percy, Freddie spirited the butt of his cigarette into a rain barrel. Percy didn't know he'd been getting them from the Meierson boys, and Gus would have been sorely disappointed if he knew.

"Gus ain't home, son. He's out looking for you. Where you been, fella? We're all worried about you."

Freddie knew Percy worried only about himself, but he

approached anyway. "I was talking to Brady Meierson. His folks got home tonight," he added, knowing he wasn't allowed to visit without their parents at home, *not that it mattered to Freddie whether Percy approved or not.* Besides, he knew Percy's mind. He knew what Percy was after. And wasn't interested in hearing it again.

"Remember the job you got," Percy ignored his explanation of *where he'd been,* as Freddie knew he would. In fact, *Percy didn't care.*

"I remember."

"The Petersons are coming in a few days. *We talked about that.* Remember?"

Freddie remembered. "I remember," he replied. It was Tuesday evening—*he'd been putting the job off, so he had little time to prepare.* He'd have to *take care* of the boat in a day or two. *"I remember,"* he cast his eyes about, his heart not in the mission.

"They can't be allowed to get to the cabin. *Don't forget that.* With them papers they're carrying, Gus will lose everything. You don't want Gus to *lose* everything, do you?"

Freddie didn't want that. Gus was his friend.

"You know what they'll do with them papers."

Freddie didn't know about any papers or what might be done with them. He suspected *there were no papers,* but he nodded anyway.

"—So you gotta be sure."

Freddie *wasn't* sure, but he said he was.

Percy's drive to recruit the boy peaked when revealing to him that Roxanne's grandfather was "…cheated by the Snelling brothers," and how "...the old man was *stopped cold by Snelling strongmen...*" when he tried financing a mill near Berry Falls. Then he recalled how Eb and Cyrus fought in the men's room of the Koochiching county court house "...because Eb spoke the truth..." about Cyrus's philandering, and how of Cyrus broke the door to the stall that Eb sought refuge in, and broke his own toe in the bargain; so when the sheriff arrived and saw what had happened, "...*Eb was charged with assault,* while Cyrus limped free."

With Cyrus's reputation for bribing officials, and *with gossip gleaned by Freddie from Ash River neighbors who were willing to talk about it,* Percy's tales rang true. But Percy's crowning achievement had the Petersons selling the boys an apartment building in the cities, *a building due to be torn down in a year.* And if he—*Percy*—hadn't stepped in with some *legitimate* property, they'd have lost everything. *And where were the boys now,* he followed, implying that Ted and the Petersons were involved in a conspiracy too harsh to be real.

Freddie was impressionable; so Percy's tales were believable up to the day Ted's *evil* sister appeared. Despite traveling north with her family *every* year, Percy argued that she despised Roxanne for the disgrace Zita brought to the Snelling family, claiming Roxy as an *outsider* interested only in Gus's money; he further insisted that she was bringing papers supporting Snelling claims to the landing which Ted was taking to his attorneys in the cities, *a trip that must be stopped at all cost.*

Percy's arguments had a hollow appeal: Mary *did* dislike Roxanne, but it was with tempered sympathy and with a compassion drawn from the conviction that Roxanne had had a bad start.

And Ted's trip was no mystery. *Everyone* knew *where* he was headed. News was scarce up north, so everyone's plans and community events were readily discussed, and Ted's itinerary was no exception.

But thanks to Freddie's snooping in the mailroom, Ted's *real* agenda was *discovered;* and it was so played upon by Percy, his charges against Ted and Mary so marbled with exaggerations, that Freddie had neither choice nor chance to think clearly. So when Neal approached him on Thursday with the Petersons' unexpected arrival, his reactions were automatic. Instead of relaying Neal's message to Gus, the need to prevent Ted's sister from reaching the cabin gathered urgency. Sabotaging the boat and motor was a hurried-up job and done without reflection. Neither Ted nor the Petersons mattered just then, only that their plans be interrupted.

Freddie had no illusions about Percy: even if Gus supported him, Freddie saw inconsistencies and an evil in Percy he often found in the faces of his street friends. But he forced from his mind the worst suspicions, fighting them off like the surreal characters of a cartooned nightmare.

After drilling a small hole above the water line near the floor planking of Ted's big wooden boat, then rigging the engine to stall when running hot and slow, Freddie wandered off to let chips fall where they may.

Freddie Moore didn't know Keith and Jeremy, nor did he care about them or about *anyone* except Gus and Max. But by befriending the kids when he did, he ran into some good fortune, for with Jeremy's disclosure at Donnavan Marsh that he'd put *them* into harm's way, and that Ted was their uncle (Freddie never found Ted mean or disagreeable), he finally came to his senses. Taking action, he returned to the landing to fix the damage done earlier in the day. But fearing being sent back to the cities if caught repairing the boat and motor, Freddie resorted to the next best thing: grabbing binoculars and extra life jackets, he started up a rental craft and headed for the narrows to assume the role of the solitary fisherman the Petersons spotted on their way out.

Chapter 11

"*Then* what, Uncle Ted?" Keith munched wide-eyed on toast and jam, as Rangers Charlie Whitcomb and Earl Morris looked on. Charlie was big and brusque with bushy brows and a head of close-cropped salt-and-pepper that defied style. Standing at the counter with a grin on his face, he overshadowed his partner whose eyes were as wide as Keith's, the same glow of excitement, *his* first big case, too. "What *did* you do, Uncle Ted?"

"Well, big fella," his uncle's clothes still damp and rumpled from the night before, "when we hit shore it was dark, and we needed protection. With that *norther* wound up like it does, that whole rock face gets washed over," his lean face a picture of adventure, his voice hushed and slow, "So we worked along into the trees…."

Moving his hands as if painting a picture within his nephew's imaginations, Ted told his story at the table where, like a bad dream, he was held captive hours earlier. With hot coffee at hand, he sat with his sister and the kids, while the rest stood by.

Meanwhile, Neal and Becky were awakened early, notified of Ted's *misadventure*, how Freddie turned himself in, and how Roxanne was arrested and under scrutiny, her story to be matched against Percy's contradictions. Bets were that despite finger pointing, neither Percy's worming nor Roxy's whining would withstand the other's sellout, and that *truth* would surface like scum on Lame Duck Pond; and no matter that Roxy's role as murderess might be limited, even her most sympathetic friends and Percy's strongest supporters must succumb to the awful evidence: that the attorney, Jenny, and the Currie boys were gone forever, and that Ted and Gus, and *even Ted's family* were targeted to join them.

"Course, we couldn't see *nothin'* out there, what with tripping over branches and boulders; and *we needed a fire* because Percy was in bad shape, the way he takes care of himself. He was wet and had the shakes real bad and was the worst for wear by then."

Avoiding Percy being ten years younger or wet cigarettes or needing a shot of gin, Ted was sincere, genuinely compassionate. Despite his weaknesses, or how he'd disposed of Jenny or the boys or that young attorney—*or what Percy's plans were for him*—his adversary needed help: Ted would have helped *Attila the Hun* if in trouble. This was difficult for friends to understand because, *like Gus*, Ted was forever forgiving, a hopelessly sympathetic product of his environment. *Like Gus,* he would turn the other cheek even at his own peril, as it had happened in the past....

One evening, as chance had it, the wind was gusting to forty as it did in November and was looking for trouble. The waves were high, and the sleet driving hard, when a call came in from near Bald Island, an acre-square, water-level protrusion with few trees, and little vegetation. Ted knew the man in peril, an upstart and local thief who'd assaulted Roxanne before Percy's re-arrival and insulted Jenny on prior occasions, a known drunk and womanizer who'd spent his last evening in a pub near the station and who'd frequently disregarded the weather. He was alone, intoxicated, and out of gas when his call came through, his boat foundering; and it was dark. Prudence prohibited a rescue, but to stay behind was unthinkable; to deny assistance was out of the question. Without hesitation, Ted struggled to his boat and headed out over the waves to assist the agitator reportedly on his way to Iron Bay. Arriving at the island too late to help, he found the overturned craft; but it took a week for the *rounder's* body to show up in the reeds a mile away.

"Anyway, we make the trees and follow this ravine a ways. The whole peninsula's a pattern of gullies, and at the end of this one-of-'em's a washed-out cave, *a bear's den* at one time." he leaned in confidence toward his nephew.

"A *bear's* den?"

"You just stumbled onto it?" Mary asked as Earl stood open-mouthed, while Keith marveled that his uncle's adventures took place while he was sleeping—*and right under his nose.*

"No, we never 'stumbled' on it. We picked berries there last summer—that government strip along the channel where the rangers run a tourist trail, and where that grocery worker fell off a stump and broke his leg, and—"

"He was showing off for his *new* bride," Charlie smiled.

"That bread truck driver…"

"You stayed in a cave? A real bear's den, Uncle Ted?"

"…Who was married twice," Mary recalled.

"That's right, young man."

"Twice? *At the same time?"* Jeremy brightened.

"No, but…*the same woman,"* her father revealed.

"And *she* had to run for help," her mother added.

"Really?" the young ranger mouthed.

"As long as that 'norther' kept pounding away—"

"At the same time?" her eyes re-widened.

"Hah!" Ted twisted around as Earl struggled to follow; then to his nephew, "All we could do was build a fire and stay warm. I didn't figure…"

"No, dear. They were divorced and remarried. *Their second honeymoon."*

"Their *what?"* Earl rejoined.

"…A search party to come looking," Ted followed as if *days ago* instead of last night.

"Couldn't have been much of a honeymoon…," the ranger mumbled.

"How'd you build a fire? And dry matches?"

"...Broken leg and all."

"Waterproof case like your dad has," Ted produced a snap-top container as the other conversation thickened. "A woodsman never leaves home without one. You pack it with paraffin paper and matches—*or his map and compass,*" he added, rejecting the new direction-finding equipment *modern* woodsmen were adopting, arguing they were ill-prepared for *real* emergencies and that old-timers could *still* teach them some things, although Ted wasn't much older than Owen or Charlie. "And that's something for *you* to remember up here," he slipped the case into Keith's shirt pocket.

"But with the wind up and no chance for signal smoke, how'd you get found on those rocks and...w*hat a long shot.* Who'd be looking? *And what time* was that?" Owen realized their paths must have crossed.

"That's right. We'd never thought to search there—or *anywhere*—but for what the kid said this morning."

"*—and Ted's radio report.*"

"*'The kid'?*" Mary started.

"*His report?*"

"That's right. *Last night.*"

"But with Percy watching him, Ted *couldn't* have—"

"Oh...not *what* he said. It's what Ted *didn't* say that troubled Earl. You see, we weren't looking for your brother when we swung by—"

"Then who—"

"What *didn't* you say?" Jeremy pushed.

"'Swing by'? *Down at the dock?*"

Jeremy scowled.

"That's right, son. *Right here,*" he thumped the cupboard countertop.

"Middle of the night?"

"'Middle of the night.'"

"I knew it I *knew* I heard something " Keith's eyes danced. "And *our great watch dog* never even woke up," at which Dusty retreated to the radio room.

"About midnight we get a call—"

"Gus's place?"

"That's right...all upset because Freddie was gone, and—"

"*Still* gone? *Midnight?* Wasn't that unusual?" Mary recalled Gus's concern and Jeremy's observations yesterday afternoon.

"*Absolutely.* This is no place for some green kid to run loose." His reply was suspiciously mild, for despite *appearances*, Freddie had turned very courageous last night.

"You were looking for *Freddie?*"

"We weren't worried about your uncle, young lady."

"No reason to be—" Ted grumped.

"Until his boat turns missing. We saw *you* folks arrived, so we figured Ted left early. Anyway, we get a report *this morning* that the kid's at the landing. *But that's it.*"

"What do you mean, *'that's it'?*"

"Well, when Gus called, we find out Ted's not been seen."

"So...why *should* he be—?"

"So...where's his boat?"

"Oh."

"The kid's O.K., but *Ted's* gone!"

"I'm gone a lot," a sheepish reply.

Charlie continued, "No reason, no word. One time his radio's down and we missed him for days."

"We decide against botherin' you folks 'till daylight," his partner followed. "We figured he'd show up."

"*And he did* " Keith triumphed.

"Thanks to Freddie."

"'*Freddie'?*" Mary turned.

"Sure. When he saw Percy was up to no good—"

"But he was—"

"—*better late than never.*"

"Wasn't he *afraid* to talk?"

"'Bout *what?*" Keith tried.

"Could have been; but 'bout daylight, they were right where he said they'd be: Ted on one rock and Percy on another."

"Well...we're glad it worked out; but...you knew *all along* how Percy was operating. So why not just jump in 'an—"

"Sure. We all *knew*, but no case against him...a *slippery* weasel."

"Like a fox?" Keith tried.

"*You're* a fox," Jeremy mumbled.

"A *young* fox, maybe—" Charlie smiled.

"A *dumb* fox."

"So, our Justice Department was bringing it together, *like a magic show,*" he snapped his fingers.

"*Like magic*'," Keith repeated.

"That's where Ted was headed—*until Percy found out.*"

"Found out *what?*"

"His phony meeting."

"*Phony*'?"

"He didn't want the whole world to know."

Whole world, indeed, Mary's thought. *Who could possibly care about his doctor's appointment?*

Obliviously, the ranger told of Ted's assistance in unraveling Percy's practices, admitting there was no board meeting at all.

"But he's run off before," she offered, deflated, but relieved she'd kept his *health problems* to herself.

"It's what he *wanted* people to think."

Privately, she brooded.

"We knew Percy was waiting for his chance—*and sure enough,* Freddie was screening Ted's mail."

His partner confirmed, "Freddie hit the jackpot."

"What 'jackpot'?" Keith tried.

"The letter he lifted—"

"About his meeting?" Owen guessed.

"What 'meeting'?"

"*Exactly!*"

"We'd have warned Ted—"

"*If we knew,*" Earl followed. "But when *we* got word, he was *already* on a limb."

"Well, I'd say *Percy's* 'on a limb'," Mary's ego mended.

"Jeremy's on a limb."

"You're a limb."

"But why *Freddie*? Did he pay the boy?"

"Well, he *gave* him things...filled his head with lies—"

"*What* lies?" Jeremy looked troubled.

"Well...how your mom and I were after Gus's land. A *terrible* story."

"Did Freddie *realize* Percy was out here?"

"Well, there's that hole in my boat—."

"And that engine job," Owen added.

"But...his *real* plans and the Currie boys...*and all that?*"

"No. Greenwall convinced him that you and Ted were no good, so—"

"He knew what to do," Ted admitted.

"What *did* he do?" Jeremy wondered. "You mean...*he drilled that hole?*"

"Was that *before* he showed us the ducks?" Keith caught on as he quietly poked his sister.

"Yes, but he didn't know who we were," a rare display of patience. Then to the group, "He didn't know us right away." She avoided *Donavan Marsh* because her parents would be upset—*and Keith knew it*. But he held quiet.

"When he realized you two might get hurt—"

"*That's* why he was in such a big hurry—*to fix the boat.*"

"Except with no time for repairs, he grabbed life jackets and headed for the narrows. When he saw your uncle in trouble, he made sure they made shore, then went back to report it."

"So, he *turned* on Percy," Owen offered.

"He was never on his side."

"What about Roxanne?" Mary started.

"We don't know. But when they're in separate rooms—"

"With murder charges."

"We'll see who breaks."

"But what was it Uncle Ted *didn't* say?" Jeremy finally repeated, determined to have her answer. "You said, 'it's what he *didn't* say' on the radio that made you suspicious, that made you start worrying…that made you come out here *at all* last night," her attention refocused on Charlie Whitcomb.

"Yes, I did, young lady, and it was something Percy didn't notice, because he didn't know your Uncle Ted and Aunt Jenny like us old-timers did. Earl here almost missed it," he pointed, his partner nodding sheepishly. "You see, every night after Ted makes his radio report—*and he's been doing that for over five years, now*—he follows it up with a little…*farewell,*" the ranger softened. "And we listen for it," he looked at Ted. "Without darned good reason, he'd never forget to say, *'Good Night, Jenny'*."

NORMANDALE COMMUNITY COLLEGE
LIBRARY
9700 FRANCE AVENUE SOUTH
BLOOMINGTON, MN 55431-4399